Miracle at Willowcreek

Miracle at Willowcreek

by

Annette LeBox

Illustrations by
Kasia Charko

SECOND STORY Press

CANADIAN CATALOGUING IN PUBLICATION DATA

LeBox, Annette
Miracle at Willowcreek

ISBN 1-896764-04-5

I. Title

PS 8573.E3364M57 1998 jC813'.54 C98-930767-0
PZ7.L42Mi 1998

Edited by Sarah Silberstein Swartz
Cover and illustrations by Kasia Charko

Second Story Press gratefully acknowledges the assistance of the Ontario Arts Council and the Canada Council for the Arts for our publishing program. We acknowledge the financial support of the Government of Canada through the Book Publishing Industry Development Program for our publishing activities.

Printed and bound in Canada

Published by
SECOND STORY PRESS
720 Bathurst Street, Suite 301
Toronto Canada M5S 2R4

For my son, Christian.
And for those who love the polder.

The crane is a powerful spirit for girls.
Those honoured by this spirit are particularly
gifted with handiwork.

— adapted from an oral history told by Old Pierre,
from *The Faith of a Coast Salish Indian,*
Diamond Jenness, ethnographer.

Contents

Acknowledgements

I WOULD LIKE TO thank my partner, Michael Sather, for opening my eyes to the natural world. Much of my knowledge of birds and their habitat has been due to his constant and patient teaching. Appreciation is also due the Alouette Field Naturalists, and, in particular, to Wilma Robinson and Ken Thomson for their willingness to answer my endless questions about cranes and to critique the novel.

Thanks to Sue Ann Alderson of the University of British Columbia Creative Writing Department for fertilizing the seed of the novel that began in her "Writing for Children" class.

I would also like to acknowledge the following individuals for reading and commenting on the manuscript: George Archibald of the International Crane Foundation for his assistance with the technical aspects of crane behaviour and to Terry Glavin and the following members of the Katzie First Nations: Debbie Miller, Richard Pierre, Agnes Pierre, Laura Williams, and Moira Adams. I am grateful to the Katzie for giving me permission to weave their traditional stories throughout the novel.

Thanks, also, to Lisa Freeman of Pitt Meadows for helping in my research of blueberry farming and to Alison Acheson, Gayle Friesen, Barbara Nickel, Christy Dunsmore, and Terry Millikan for their insightful comments.

Many scholarly works inspired and informed parts of the narrative. Of these the most important were the writings of crane researchers and naturalists, such as Lawrence Walkinshaw, Dayton O. Hyde, Steve Grooms, Paul A. Johnsgard and Aldo

Leopold as well as the innovative experiments in isolation rearing by Dr. Rob Horwich. *You Are Asked To Witness: The Stó:lō in Canada's Pacific Coast History*, edited by Keith Thor Carlson, also proved informative.

Raising Crane, the award-winning documentary by filmmaker Dave Erickson of Spring Green, Wisconsin, gave me a deeper understanding of the special bond between the inter-species foster parent and the crane chicks.

Thanks to illustrator, Kasia Charko, for capturing the magic of the polder with such care and accuracy. A special thanks to Margie Wolfe, Karen Farquhar, Liz Martin, Beth McAuley, and Lois Pike of Second Story Press and to my editor Sarah Swartz for her advice and assistance. Her understanding of the novel's themes and meticulous attention to detail helped me to sharpen and refine my vision.

I am grateful to the Canada Council for providing me with a travel grant to the Jasper-Pulaski Management Area in Indiana to research the greater sandhill cranes, and also to the Saskatchewan Writers' and Artist's Colony at St. Peter's Abbey for providing a quiet and meditative space for me to work.

꩜

· I ·

Willowcreek Farm

GAROO-A-A-A! Tess woke to the song of the cranes. It was a pair of sandhills singing to one another across the marsh.

She jumped out of bed and ran to the window. Then she saw them! Huge silver birds with crimson crests flying past her window. So close she imagined reaching out and stroking their beautiful feathers. Their wing span was immense, at least two metres, and their long slender legs trailed behind them like streamers.

Garoooooo tuk tuk tuk, sang the crane pair. Tess shivered as the crane song rang through the stillness of the morning. The music was a haunting sound with many variations: bells tumbling down a grassy slope or trumpets announcing an important event. At other times, it sounded like a troop of clumsy clowns dropping marbles on a polished floor or ghosts shaking strange wooden rattles.

The birds soared in the updrafts for several minutes, then disappeared into the hardhack bushes lining the creek.

I saw the cranes today, Grandpa, whispered Tess.

She closed the bedroom window and curled up in the old wicker chair. In the distance, she could see the mist floating above the water of the slough, but beyond that — nothing. Not the row of cottonwoods lining the slough or the bog forests creeping up the mountains — not even the mountains themselves.

She grabbed a quilt from the foot of her bed and pulled it around her shoulders. April in the Pitt Polder seemed colder than Toronto. She knew that wasn't true, but it felt like it to her. It was the dampness that surprised her, a dampness that settled deeply into her bones.

The summers she'd spent at Willowcreek Farm in Pitt Meadows were hot. She'd slept with the window open, grateful for the slough breezes and the summer downpours. Every morning with backpacks filled with bird books and binoculars, a spotting scope and flasks of hot chocolate, she and Grandpa would go birding in the marsh. They'd wait until dawn for a glimpse of the greater sandhill cranes — birds her grandfather once called the shyest creatures on earth.

Grandpa had loved the sandhills. He'd known the location of every nest in the polder, their favourite roosting spots, the number of singles and mated pairs. Last year, he'd counted only twenty cranes in the entire polder. There had been twenty-five the year before. That's why he'd watch each nest with such anticipation. The cranes were so close to extinction that any addition to the dwindling family seemed a cause for celebration. Later, after Tess had returned to Toronto, he'd watch the young cranes fly south. And when he'd hear the first cries of the sandhills in the spring, he'd phone Tess with the news.

"The cranes are back!" he'd say, laughing, and she'd cross the months off on her calendar: April, May, June. Until she'd wave goodbye to her mother and fly to Vancouver, British Columbia. Then Grandpa would pick her up at the airport and they'd drive east for forty-six kilometres until they reached Pitt Meadows. A short drive from the small town, to the northeast, lay the Pitt Polder, at one time, almost entirely covered in water. Before Tess was born, these wetlands had been drained and dyked by Dutch pioneers like her great-grandfather, Jan De Boer, so they could farm. The farmland and the surrounding wetlands surrounding were called a "polder," a Dutch word meaning "land reclaimed from the sea." And right in the centre of the polder, surrounded by miles of winding creeks that Grandpa called sloughs, sat Willowcreek Farm, Grandpa's home, and now hers.

I wish you were here, Grandpa. I thought I loved Willowcreek. But I was wrong. It wasn't the place that was special. It was you. I've been here five days and I haven't left the house. Can you imagine? Me staying inside? But if you were here, you'd say, 'The sandhills are singing. Go find them.'

She picked up her bird notebook lying on her dresser. Grandpa had given it to her that first summer on the polder. But since Grandpa had died, she hadn't touched it. She hesitated for a moment, then took the pencil from its sheath attached to the small notebook, and began to write.

April 13, 5:45 a.m. Willowcreek farmhouse

2 sandhill cranes flying over the farmhouse. Their feathers were silver. No sign of rust so they haven't painted themselves yet. I wonder if they're a pair. Or maybe they are bachelors, too young to mate. Were they calling to one another or to neighbouring pairs across the marsh? So many questions and no one to answer them.

Grandpa, I miss you. I wonder if you know how much. Why didn't you tell me you were sick? Why didn't Mom? I never had a chance to say goodbye.

She blinked back tears. Why did her mother bring her here? She wanted to go home. But there was nothing left there. Her mother had sold everything, except their clothes and her precious sewing machine.

She glanced at her suitcase laying open in the centre of the floor. She pulled out some thick woolen socks, jeans, a warm sweater, and a raincoat. Dressing quickly, she grabbed her binoculars and her notebook and tiptoed down the hall. As she walked past the next bedroom, she caught a glimpse of her mother curled up in her grandfather's bed.

She could hear Uncle Randall's snoring in the next room. She held her breath as she tiptoed past the closed door. Thank goodness her uncle was a sound sleeper.

Outside, Tess scanned the early morning sky. No cranes in sight — only the mist rising and falling like floating islands. Tess held out her hand to see if it was raining. Then she lifted her face to catch the raindrops on her tongue. A marsh rain was like loneliness: too fine to see, but you could feel it.

Passing through the back garden, she caught the scent of lilacs. She stopped for a moment, buried her face in the blossoms, then followed a cobbled path lined with tulips on either side — bulbs her great-grandfather had brought from Holland. At the end of the garden, Tess opened a gate and began walking across the field. With each step, her feet sank into thick black mud. It's spring, she reminded herself, not mid-summer. By then the bright green of this soggy field would dry a brilliant gold and the meadows would be heavy with the fragrance of honeysuckle and swamp rose.

Tess raised her binoculars, searching the field. As long as the cranes remained still, their protective colouring would make it difficult to distinguish them from their surroundings. She adjusted the focus and checked the sweet gale bushes near the slough ditch. The cranes might hide there. But she saw only the bright yellow feathers of some yellowthroats flitting from branch to branch. *Witchety-witchety-witchety*, they sang.

She stopped to count them. Then she pulled out her notebook and hastily added the entry.

8 yellowthroats on the sweet gale bushes behind the house.

She walked to the end of the field, passed through a rickety gate that led to a salmonberry thicket. In the distance, she heard a faint yipping sound. Coyote! She and Grandpa had often come across them. Grandpa liked to talk coyote in a soft voice. The animal would stare at them for several minutes before running across the fields. With Grandpa beside her, she hadn't been afraid. But facing a coyote by herself was different.

Skirting the brambles, Tess plowed her way through knee-high grass to the base of a steep slope. From there she climbed to the dyke road.

Standing on the road, she looked down on the slough.

Willowcreek, she whispered, but the word caught in her throat. She'd stood on this spot for the first time five years ago. She was seven then and she'd hardly known her grandfather. But he'd held her hand as he told her stories of how the dykes were built. Her great-grandfather had helped build the dyke road she was standing on. The farmers used horse-drawn plows to dig up miles and miles of ditches. Then they used the earth to build high walls to hold back the waters of the marsh. Later, they built roads on top of the dykes. Some farmers chose to raise cattle, others corn and hay. The De Boers had chosen to grow blueberries.

Tess's summers were spent picking blueberries and birding. How she had loved Willowcreek then.

Suddenly the wind picked up, sending the willows and the marsh grass swaying. She saw two beady eyes peering down at her from a bare branch of the cottonwood. It was a mature bald eagle, its white neck feathers ruffling in the wind.

A flock of red-winged blackbirds riding on some cattails began to shriek, *Kong-ka-ree, kong-ka-ree!*

Tess sensed something shifting. She pulled down her hood and searched the area with her binoculars. She could no longer see the farmhouse because of the mist. Then she saw something moving by the dyke road. But it wasn't a crane.

It looked like a figure wearing a brown hood. The figure floated through the mist, like a ghost with the fog rising round, the face hidden in the shadows of the hood. She shuddered and crouched down into the long grass.

But when she looked again, the figure was gone.

Tess shook her head. Had she imagined it? It couldn't have disappeared. There were no bushes nearby.

The rain was making soft pinging noises on the marsh grass. Droplets formed on her lashes. She kept wiping her eyes and looking in every direction. But the mist had grown thicker. Now she could see no more than a few feet around her.

Ahead, a flock of blackbirds shrieked out. Were they sending a warning?

Tess felt her mouth go dry.

Something was rustling in the grass. She held her breath. It couldn't be cranes. They'd never come that close.

Then suddenly, she thought she saw the shadowy form again. It was on the dyke road. She felt her chest tighten. She walked faster, then ran. She glanced back. The figure was following her! Quickly. Back towards the house. No time to pick her way through the dry spots of the boggy field. She stumbled down the sharp incline of the dyke, past the brambles and across the field.

Keep moving. Don't look back. She thought she heard someone calling her name. Remember the patch of devil's club. Sharp prickly spines. Avoid those. There it was. In front of her. Go round it.

She tripped over a tree root. Felt herself falling. The next moment, she was lying face down in the wet grass.

· 2 ·

Birds of a Feather

TESS BLINKED. She wiped the grass from her eyes and looked around. Her ankle hurt. She heard footsteps behind her.

Uncle Randall.

"And pray tell, young lady, what are you doing?" asked her uncle in a loud voice. He was wearing a dull black raincoat with a small cape jutting out from the shoulders and a black rain hat with a brim. He carried a walking stick with a shiny gold handle. He looked pleased to see her, like a cat who'd just caught a mouse.

"I ... I was looking for the cranes," said Tess. "I fell. The grass is wet."

"Foolish child," said her uncle. "You shouldn't be out here by yourself. You must wait until your mother accompanies you. You see what can happen?" He bent over her, clearing his throat. "Do you need help?"

"No," said Tess. "I'm fine." She picked herself up and wiped the grass off her jeans.

"Then I will accompany you back to the house," he said.

"Huh ... how did you ... find me?" asked Tess.

"I heard you sneaking down the stairs."

Tess felt colour rushing to her cheeks.

I wasn't sneaking. I heard the cranes singing and I followed them.

Uncle Randall placed his hand on her shoulder. "You can't be gallivanting half the night out on the polder, child. It's dangerous — as you can see."

"But Grandpa and I ..."

"I know *exactly* what you and your grandfather did. Watching those ... birds ... at all hours of the day and night. I did not approve of it and I told him so. But that was typical of my father. Sometimes I think he loved birds more than people."

He did not! You know he didn't. Grandpa was good to everyone.

She tried to change the subject.

"Did you see anyone else ... I mean, besides me?" she asked.

Her uncle eyed her suspiciously.

"No. Why?"

"I just wondered," replied Tess, quickly. The figure had come from the direction of the creek. It couldn't have been her uncle.

"The next time you go walking on the polder, go with your mother."

"Mom hates walking," said Tess.

The only time her mother ever went for a walk was in

the summertime and then, only if the weather was hot. If she had to wait for her mother to take her walking, she'd never see a crane!

Her uncle's stride was brisk and Tess had to walk and run a little to keep up with him. It was obvious he didn't like her. Last summer he'd hardly spoken to her and when he had, it was to remind her of her homework. Homework on the summer holidays! He was oblivious to her life.

And once she'd overheard him talking to her grandfather.

"That girl's spoiled rotten," her uncle had said. "Whatever she wants, you give her. You spend half the night taking her out on those bird-watching jaunts. You never spent that kind of time with me when I was a kid."

"You weren't interested a whit in crane-watching, Randall, and you know it!" Grandpa had told him. "You were interested in get-rich schemes: your lemonade stands and the wooden planes you tried to sell to the neighbour kids. I helped you make signs and flyers. But you took after your mother. You were both hothouse flowers. Tess is a birder. Like me."

She and Grandpa. Birds of a feather.

"I must be off now, young lady," said Uncle Randall, tipping the brim of his hat. "I've got land to sell. But take my advice. Don't go out on the polder alone."

Her uncle pointed his walking stick in the direction of the garage and followed it.

Moments later, Tess heard the car idling. She saw Uncle

Randall piling signs into the trunk of his car. Her uncle's photograph smiled up at her from the signs.

Tess read: *Pitt Polder Realty. Randall De Boer. A realtor who cares.*

No wonder her uncle always seemed in a hurry. He was doing two jobs now, growing blueberries and selling real estate. There was little to do on the farm in the winter, but in the spring, the blueberry bushes had to be pruned and the grass between the rows of bushes had to be cut. Summer was the busiest, even though Grandpa hired crews of pickers. But he always found time for birding.

As she entered the house, she heard someone in the kitchen.

"Is that you, Mom?" called out Tess.

"Not so loud," said a voice. When Tess entered she saw her mother, Marjory, sitting beside the wood stove. She was sipping a cup of coffee.

"I'm still not awake," said her mom, yawning. "Where were you, early bird?"

"I went for a walk," said Tess.

"Down by the slough?" asked Marjory.

Tess saw the alarm in her mother's eyes.

"Stop worrying, Mom."

Her mother frowned, "Please don't go out there by yourself again."

Tess didn't answer. She was staring at her mother. People always told her, "Your mother's so pretty." And this morning she could see why. Dressed in the gold and ivory silk kimono, with her perfect skin and her long painted nails and dark wavy hair, her mom looked like an exotic butterfly. Tess felt so ordinary beside her.

"Why is Uncle Randall selling real estate now?" asked Tess, warming her hands in front of the stove.

"Your uncle doesn't want to farm anymore. He wasn't cut out for it. Neither am I."

"Then why did we move here?"

"How many times do we have to go over this?" sighed her mother. "I thought you'd be thrilled. Willowcreek, Willowcreek, Willowcreek. That's all you'd talk about in Toronto ... and now you're here, you're not happy. I had two choices. Buy out Randall's share of the farm or move here and help him. And I don't have the money to buy him out. At least, not now."

"But I thought your sewing came first. How could you give it up to become a blueberry farmer?"

Marjory placed one hand on her hip. "Tess, you're exaggerating. I'm not going to become a blueberry farmer! Randall needs help with the harvest and we're going to help him. July and August will be busy, but I'll have the rest of the year to sew. And if we have a good crop of berries, we'll make enough money to get by, especially now I don't have to pay rent. I just know this is the right thing to do."

"Maybe it's right for you. You didn't leave all your friends behind."

"Really? What about Maggie and Ben? Do you think I won't miss them?"

Tess shrugged. She knew her mother left friends behind, too. She knew she was behaving badly, but the words kept popping out. Angry, mean words. Later, she knew she'd feel guilty.

"One day you love a place, the next day you hate it," said her mother. "I can't understand you."

"It's not the same here without Grandpa," said Tess.

"There's no pleasing you," said Marjory, putting her coffee cup down hard. Tess recognized the familiar tightness around her mother's mouth.

Her mother walked over to the sewing table in the corner of the kitchen. She turned the tiny light on the machine.

That's right, Mom. Go back to your sewing. That's all you ever care about.

The whirr of the sewing machine filled the kitchen.

End of conversation.

Tess went upstairs, changed into dry clothes and threw herself on the bed.

Tomorrow was Monday. Her first day of school. She'd tried to persuade her mother to let her finish her school year at Danforth Elementary School in Toronto. She could have stayed with Martine, her best friend, and her family, but her mother had insisted she transfer to Meadowland right away.

"You'll make friends," her mother had said. "Wait and see." But Tess knew how badly kids treated someone new at school.

Tess remembered Jessie, a new girl that came to Danforth three months earlier. No one was mean to her — not exactly — but the girl wasn't invited to sleepovers or parties and she always left school by herself. She had spoken to Jessie, but Tess hadn't made an effort to include her. No one had.

Now *she'd* be an outsider, like Jessie.

Tess pushed away the thought. It was too late to do anything now. She had to think about tomorrow.

She got up from the bed and began searching through her suitcase. She pulled out a dark grey mini-jumper. It was made of fine wool and lined with polyester. Her mother's own label was at the back: D. B. for De Boer. Her mother had copied the design from a photograph she'd seen in *Vogue*. Tess had only worn it once in Toronto and her friends Martine and Susan had loved it. They'd taken turns borrowing it, before she left.

"You're so lucky to have a mother that sews," they always said.

Tess tried on the jumper. She stared at herself in the mirror. The jumper looked pretty good. Then she tried on her new shoes, the latest style in the city — clunky black shoes with three-inch heels. They'd go perfectly.

She stepped back, tripping over the open suitcase lying

on the floor. She gave the case a push with her foot, then flopped onto her bed again. She may as well unpack. Willowcreek was her home now, whether she liked it or not.

·3·

Ghost

Tᴇss ᴡᴏᴋᴇ ᴡɪᴛʜ a start. She'd been dreaming of the polder ghost. It was chasing her. She felt a hand touch her shoulder. The ghost slowly removed its hood. Uncle Randall's face stared up at her, ghoulish and horrible.

It's only a dream, she told herself. She glanced at her clock. Five past three — much too early to get up for school, but she was wide awake. She pulled on her housecoat and sat by the window.

There was a ring of cloud around the moon and patches of low lying mist hovering above the fields. It would soon be dawn; if the cranes were nesting by the creek, she might be lucky enough to catch a glimpse of them.

A high-pitched wheezy cry broke the stillness. Then a short low hiss. Tess shivered.

It's probably a barn owl.

Then she saw someone walking across the back field. Was she awake or dreaming? She shook her head, trying to wake herself up. She pressed her head against the glass. Whoever it was wore a hood, its face hidden in the folds. Who or what could it be? And why was it out there?

Maybe the polder *was* haunted.

She ran down the hallway.

"Mom!" she whispered, trying not to awaken Uncle Randall. But her mother didn't stir. Tess tried again.

"Mom!"

Her mother opened her eyes, glanced at the clock, then closed her eyes with a sigh.

"It's too early, dear. Go back to bed."

"Mom ..." said Tess weakly, but her mother had already slipped back to sleep.

Her mother's face looked strained and swollen. Tess wondered whether she'd been crying. Her mother hardly ever cried, not even after Grandpa had died.

Tess reached towards her, then changed her mind. Mom reminded her of Snow White, always working or sleeping. And Tess was one of the dwarfs. Grumpy or Dopey. She smiled in spite of herself.

She crept back to her room and peered out the window. The mist had lifted, so she could see as far as the slough. The moon shone a silvery light on the surface of the water. But she saw nothing.

She grabbed the comforter from her bed and placed it over the chair by the window. Then she curled up her legs and snuggled inside. If the figure appeared again, she wanted to be ready.

When Tess woke up, her legs felt stiff and sore. She was surprised to find herself still in the chair. One leg had gone to sleep. Looking out she saw the sun was high in the sky and the mist had lifted. She glanced at the clock, then jumped up and stretched. She had only an hour to get to the bus stop. Thank goodness she'd put out her clothes the night before. She showered and dressed, ate a bowl of cereal and grabbed the bag lunch that Mom had left in the fridge and stuffed it into her backpack. Then she checked the outside pocket for her notebook. It was a habit she'd learned from Grandpa. Birds are everywhere, he'd said, if you keep your eyes and ears open.

At first, her friends in Toronto thought it strange that she'd stop on the street to list a bird in her notebook or to search through her field guide for its identity. But she told them that some kids collected baseball cards or stamps or stuffed animals. She collected bird sightings. After awhile, they started noticing birds, too.

As she walked down the laneway to the main road, she wished she hadn't worn her city shoes. The lane was muddy and full of potholes. By the time she reached Pitt Road, her new shoes were covered in mud and her feet were hurting. In Toronto, the school was only three blocks from her house and the sidewalks were clean. Tomorrow, she would wear her high-top runners.

The sun was shining and spring was in the air. She breathed in the mossy fragrance of wet grass and sword fern and clover. She walked past farm houses and rust-coloured barns and long straight rows of blueberry bushes and fields of corn stubble baked golden by last summer's sun. She walked past ditches lined with lupines and spring gold and wild chamomile.

Everywhere around her, she saw green. The deep grey-green of mountain forests, the red-green of the Labrador tea and the pale mustard-green of new grass shoots sprouting in the corn field.

In Toronto, it would be lunchtime now. If she were there, she'd be walking home for lunch with Martine. Martine was from Quebec City and her mother loved to cook, so lunch at Martine's was a treat. Tess's favourite was poutine — french fries with cheese curds, smothered with thick brown gravy. Just the thought of it made her mouth water. But Tess's mom would never make poutine. She said it was too greasy.

Tess heard a soft puttering sound from the direction of the river. She stopped in her tracks, scanning the field.

It was a pair of cranes! The birds were rooting in the mud, no more than twenty metres away. The largest crane swung its head around and flapped its wings. Then it picked up a piece of marsh grass in its beak and threw it into the air. The female flapped her wings then retrieved the grass, tossing it exactly as her mate had done.

Tess could hardly contain her excitement. Her grandfather had told her that cranes often begin to toss objects as a warm-up before dancing. She stood frozen, afraid to move a muscle. The male pecked at the ground as if searching for a different object. Finally, the bird found a stick, tossed it, then suddenly stood erect, turning the back of his out-spread wings to the female.

He's showing off, thought Tess. She crossed her fingers and held her breath.

"Dance," she whispered. "Dance! It's spring!"

But the female seemed to lose interest. She went back to searching for grubs and worms. The male stared at his mate for a few moments, then resumed his feeding.

Tess sighed. Her body felt heavy with disappointment. She'd never seen the cranes dance, though she'd watched them for five summers.

"If you see the cranes dance once in a lifetime, you are lucky," her grandfather had said.

Spring was the height of the cranes' dance season. And this was her first spring in the polder. Her first spring without Grandpa.

She stood watching the crane pair until a car went by. At the sound of the motor, the cranes took flight. She stood watching them until they disappeared from view.

You promised that one day I'd see them. Remember, Grandpa? You promised.

Turning her sights to the road, she glimpsed the bright orange of the school bus in the distance.

She began to run, wobbling on her high heels. She could feel a blister forming on one heel. City shoes! What a mistake!

When she reached the bus stop, she was out of breath.
She saw seven or eight kids staring at her.

"You didn't have to run," said a boy about her age. "The driver's probably waiting for the McNarney kids. They're always late." The boy was wearing jeans and a plaid shirt. He would have looked exactly right sitting on a tractor.

"You're new around here, aren't you?" asked the boy.

Tess nodded.

"I'm Zak," he said. "That's Rowena and that's Gail." Rowena was tall and thin with sharp features and Gail was short with small piercing eyes.

"Hello," said the girls. They gave Tess suspicious looks.

"What grade are you in?" asked the boy.

"Seven," said Tess.

"Hey! You'll be in our class," said Zak. Rowena and Gail frowned. Then Tess heard a giggle. Rowena was pointing at Tess's feet.

"Where did you get those shoes?" she asked.

Tess stared at her feet.

"Toronto."

"Weird," said Gail with a smirk.

The two girls burst into laughter.

Tess flinched.

Rowena had long brown hair and small round darting eyes, like a cowbird. Gail had a crop of freckles and bright red hair. Ruby-crowned kinglet. No. The ruby crowns were too sweet. Sapsucker was more like it. Sharp-beaked and saucy!

Tess and Grandpa had played the bird game — associating people with their bird types — the first summer she'd come to Willowcreek. They'd been caught in a downpour while they were birding and they'd taken shelter in a hollow trunk of a huge cedar tree. The game had lasted till the rain stopped. They'd decided that Mom was a trumpeter swan, because she had a long neck and was beautiful. Tess had said that Uncle Randall was a kingfisher, because he had a loud voice and liked to preen. He wore a white shirt and blue suit and had black bushy hair that stuck out in weird places.

"Don't be saucy," said Grandpa, then he chuckled a little.

"Saucy" was one of Grandpa's favourite words, along with "persnickety." They both meant the same thing, but persnickety was worse than saucy. Sometimes Tess felt persnickety inside, though she tried to hide it. The cowbird and sapsucker were staring at her. Tess pulled up her hood and stood facing the other way.

The boy came over to her. "Ignore them," he said. "They'll be okay once they get to know you."

Who wants to know them? That's what she wanted to say. But she didn't, of course.

The bus was almost full when Tess got on, except for several seats close to the driver.

Tess sat in the first window seat and Zak slid in beside

her. He gave her a quick smile and she felt her cheeks grow hot. A girl wearing a beadwork choker joined them. She had a moon-shaped face and large laughing eyes.

"Hi, Sally," said Zak.

The girl waved at Zak and nodded at Tess.

Rowena and Gail sat in the seat across from them. Tess could hear them giggling and whispering.

"Charlie Nevin saw the polder ghost last night," said Gail.

Tess started. Maybe she hadn't been dreaming.

"Tell Zak, ghostbuster of the polder!" said Rowena loudly.

"Tell me what?" asked Zak.

"Old Charlie saw the ghost last night," said Rowena.

"Where did he see it?" asked Zak, sitting forward.

"Near the slough behind our house," said Gail. "I overheard him telling my dad this morning. Charlie woke us all up, banging on our door. I asked Dad about it over breakfast, but he wouldn't say much more. He said the mist plays tricks on people."

"What was Charlie doing on the polder?" asked Zak.

"Fishing in the slough, probably," said Gail. "When I saw him in our kitchen, he looked scared. His hands were shaking."

"Proves my point, Row," said Zak. "How many more sightings do you need to admit there's a ghost out there? Everyone can't be imagining it!"

"I'm not convinced," said Rowena coldly.

"What does the ghost look like?" asked Tess.

Suddenly Tess felt everyone's eyes on her.

"Why?" asked Rowena. Tess heard dislike in the girl's voice. She instantly regretted having spoken.

"I ... uh ... saw someone walking on the polder this morning ... from my bedroom window. I couldn't see the face. Whoever it was wore a hood and a long coat. It looked as if it was floating, then disappeared into thin air."

"Another sighting!" said Zak. "I think we should go ghost-hunting!"

"Don't look at me," said Sally.

"Come on, Sally. It'll be fun."

"I don't fool around with spirits. Ask Robby to go with you."

"He plays soccer all weekend," said Zak. "Besides, he wouldn't be interested." He turned to Tess. "Hey, city girl, why don't you come?"

"Me?" Tess felt her cheeks colour. He was cute and he seemed nice, too.

"Sure. Row ... you and Gail are invited, too."

"Who's going?" asked Rowena, raising her eyebrows.

"Tess and Sally — if I can persuade them — and me."

"Tess and Sally?"

"And you and Gail."

"I don't think so," said Rowena. She looked angry.

Gail didn't say anything.

Sally leaned towards Tess and whispered, "What time did you see the ghost?"

"A little after three this morning. I heard the cry of a barn owl and ran to the window to see it."

Sally shuddered.

"Do you know," said Sally quietly, "that a ghost sometimes takes on the form of a small owl."

"Really?" whispered Tess.

"Yes! And the owl haunts the place where a person first receives their guardian spirit. The owl spends most of the night hunting, but its feeding time is around three in the morning. The exact time you saw it!"

"You made that up, right?" said Tess, quietly.

"No, it's true. My grandfather says it is, anyway."

"What does the ghost feed on?"

"I don't know and I don't want to find out," said Sally.

Giggles erupted from the seat across from them. Rowena must have overheard.

"Sally's telling stories again," said Rowena in a mock-scary voice.

"Mind your own business," said Sally.

"Where's her moccasins?" whispered Rowena, just loud enough for Sally to hear.

Tess looked at Sally's eyes. She saw hurt.

Rowena the Mean. You think it's okay to put someone down. Well, its not.

Rowena caught Tess looking at her. "What's your

problem, city girl?"

Tess didn't answer. She stared down at her muddy shoes. If only she could close her eyes, click her heels together and be back home in Toronto.

She looked out the window and watched the passing scenery. The day seemed too beautiful to feel sad, but she couldn't shake the feeling.

Across a deep blue sky, she saw a flock of Canada geese winging towards the mountains. Five ... ten ... fifteen, maybe sixteen.

Honk! Honk! Honk! they called.

"Take me with you," she whispered as she watched them grow smaller and smaller, until finally, they disappeared.

· 4 ·

Uncle Randall's Project

FRIDAY AT LAST! Tess breathed a sigh of relief as she entered the kitchen.

"Hi, Mom," said Tess.

Her mother was bent over her sewing machine.

"Wait till I finish this seam," said Marjory, without looking up.

Tess placed her backpack down and grabbed a cookie. Her first week of school was over, but she had nothing planned for the weekend. If she were in Toronto, she and Martine would have a sleepover or go to a party, or they'd meet for coffee at The Coffee Bean. Her mother didn't know she drank coffee. If she had known, she'd say Tess wasn't old enough, even though her mom drank coffee all the time. But you couldn't really belong to the group, if you didn't drink coffee. Coffee drinking was a big part of it.

Tess wondered if Rowena and Gail drank coffee.

She poured herself some juice and took another cookie. Marjory was working on a dress sleeve. Tess hated sewing sleeves. She always had trouble getting them to fit right on the shoulders. Her mother would need at least five minutes to finish. At least.

Tess heard some house finches warbling outside. She opened the window and stuck out her head.

Pshhh, pshhh, pshhh, she called.

The finches let out a series of high-pitched chirps.

"Close that window," said her mother. "It's freezing in here."

Tess shut the window and pulled her notebook from her pocket.

Leaning on her elbows, she peered through the window, noting the intricate details of the birds — the deep rose-coloured feathers, the tiny eye stripes, the notches on the tail, the small black moustache below the beak. Her grand-father had taught her to notice the details — to see and to hear like a birder. Grandpa had worn glasses and was a little hard of hearing, but he paid attention more. She took out her pencil and began to write.

April 18, 4:00 p.m. Maple tree outside the kitchen window

4 house finches. 3 males and 1 female. Small birds. The males have a brown cap and a dark moustache below the beak. The feathers on their bibs are red and they have a red stripe above the eye. Their rump feathers are also red. I used to think the rump was the tail feathers, but it's the feathers on the back of the bird, just before the tail feathers begin.

*The males are so pretty! The females are a streaky
brown, much plainer. I wonder why the males are
usually brighter? Is that wheer sound their song or
their call? I must look it up in Grandpa's field guide.
But looking at his things makes me sad.*

"Finished," said her mother, shutting off the sewing
machine light. Then she added, "I have some great news!"

"What?"

"I put an ad in the paper and I've got two customers
already. One woman wants me to make her wedding gown
and bridesmaids' dresses and the other wants me to design
some resort wear. She's going to Hawaii. Apparently, there's
no one in Pitt Meadows that designs clothing, as well as
sews. If they're satisfied with my work, they'll tell all their
friends."

"They'll be satisfied," said Tess.

"I suppose so," said Marjory. "We could use the
money." Then her mother's face brightened. "If we get a
good crop of blueberries this summer and I get some steady
sewing work, we'll get by. So how did your first week of
school go?"

"Okay," said Tess.

"Have you made any friends yet?"

"A girl called Sally. She asked me to be her partner in
math," said Tess.

Tess knew she was stretching the truth by mentioning

Sally's name. What was the use in telling her mom she'd made no friends and she hated it here. Her mother had her own worries.

"That's wonderful, dear," said Marjory. "Oh, I almost forgot. I bought a surprise for you."

"Really?"

Her mother handed Tess a remnant of pale blue fabric.

"Isn't it the prettiest print!"

"Mom!" groaned Tess.

Her mother looked disappointed. "I thought you'd like it. The material's so beautiful."

"How many times do I have to tell you? I hate sewing. I don't want to do it anymore."

"That's because you're too fussy," sighed her mom. "You think everything has to be perfect. It doesn't need to be."

"*You* wouldn't wear something that wasn't."

Marjory looked surprised. Then she laughed. "I suppose you're right. That was my own mother's doing. Everything had to be done a certain way. But it paid off. By the time I was your age, I was a skilful seamstress."

"Not me," said Tess, shaking her head.

"Yes, you, too! How many girls of twelve can say they've made their whole wardrobe!"

"It was torture," said Tess. "All those hours sitting in front of that sewing machine. All those stupid zippers put in inside out and the crooked seams and the blouses that didn't fit. I'm never doing it again!"

"Tess, you're being dramatic. It wasn't that bad and you know it. You should be proud of what you've accomplished."

I'm not like you, Mom. I'll never be like you. I hated sewing those clothes. I had to unpick those seams a million times before I got them right.

"Ready, Marjory?" called a voice from the hallway. Tess could hear the car motor running.

Her mother threw up her hands.

"Oh, dear, I completely forgot. I'll run up and get my coat. You come too, Tess."

"Where are we going?"

"For a drive. Your uncle tells me he has something exciting to show us."

Uncle Randall's car was parked outside the house. It was long, black and shiny. Tess climbed into the back. She sunk into the deep blue velour seats. The seat belt automatically snapped itself into place. Uncle Randall must be selling a lot of real estate.

She noticed her uncle was driving in the direction of the lake.

"Where are we going?" asked Tess.

"We are going to see one of the most exciting projects this area has ever known!" said her uncle in a booming voice. "Sandhill Golf Resort!"

"Where's that?" asked Tess.

"On the polder," said Uncle Randall. "Only a few miles from here. Down Pitt Road."

Tess's mouth fell open.

"But that's marsh!" said Tess. "The cranes nest there!"

"The cranes won't be harmed, dear! We've had an expert assure us of that. It's a golf course now. Nice green grass! They've done a beautiful job!"

Tess swallowed hard. A golf course. On the polder. It was hard to imagine. She wondered if Grandpa had known about it before he died. He would have hated it.

As Uncle Randall drove down Pitt Road, Tess noticed that the hardhack and sweet gale had been cut down. The bushes were the homes of marsh wrens and Virginia rails and marsh harriers and greater sandhill cranes.

How could they call the resort "Sandhill"? Cranes would never nest on a golf course. There was no cover from their enemies. There was no water.

"Look, there it is!" said Uncle Randall, pointing to a distant building high on a hill. The resort looked like a golden castle gleaming in the sunlight, but the lowlands surrounding it looked altered.

The ancient groves of alder, cottonwood, and poplar were gone. And the wild cranberries with their tart-sweet taste and the lady's slippers and the swamp lilies and wild roses, the lupines and cattails, the trilliums and buttercups — all gone. Between the trees lining the river and the road, there was nothing but grass.

Tess clutched the doorhandle of the car. She tightened her grasp as she slowly took in the scene.

The marsh was being ruined.

They drove past rows of spindly nursery trees — aspens and maples. The trees were planted alternately — an aspen, then a maple, along the edge of the golf course. The pruned and trimmed nursery trees all looked the same.

Someone must have thought the symmetry was beautiful. But she hated it. She liked the wild trees — the way they spread their limbs towards the light — each tree a different size and shape.

Then she remembered the singing tree. The old spruce was a landmark in the area. It was the largest tree for miles around. She opened the car window and stuck out her head. Had she been daydreaming and missed it?

No. It was gone, too.

She'd called it the singing tree because hundreds of pine siskins liked to sit inside its branches and sing. The chorus of birds was loud and wheezy — a rising *shr-ee, shr-ee.* She'd felt like laughing every time she'd heard it.

The first time she'd seen the tree was when she was five. She'd said, "Look, Grandpa, the tree is singing!" Her grandfather had laughed and pointed out the birds hidden within its branches. The birds were hard to spot, except for the tiny patch of yellow on their wing feathers. But the name had stuck.

The singing tree.

Uncle Randall parked the car at the edge of the golf course. He led them across the greens. The ground was spongy and wet.

Tess kicked at the grass as she walked.

Where would the siskins go now?

Uncle Randall was beaming. "What do you think, Marjory?"

"How can they build a resort here?" asked Tess's mother. "It's wetlands. It floods every spring."

"Pumps, Marjory! Huge ones! See over there. The pumps drain the water off. Works like a charm!" He rubbed his hands together. "And this is only Phase A! If we can get the land rezoned, then we'll be able to move to Phase B. We'll build a shopping mall, hotel complex, condominiums, recreation centre, marina — and last, but not least, a theme park!" Uncle Randall turned to Tess, grinning. "You won't have to go to California to see Disneyland, young lady! You'll have a theme park next door!"

But cranes can't live in a theme park. What about them?

"Maybe I should take up golf," said Marjory. "It would be a good way to meet people."

Couldn't her mother see the golf course had a cost?

"Great idea," said Randall. "I'm sure I could get you a deal on a membership." He glanced at Tess. "Maybe you'd would like to take up the game, too."

"No, thank you," said Tess coldly.

The frown line between her mother's eyebrows deepened.

"You might like it," she said. "Your uncle is only trying to be nice."

Tess winced. Her mom never took her side. At first, she thought she was imagining it, but it had happened too often. Now she expected it.

She lagged behind, making puddles by pushing her toe into the soggy ground. Golf! She couldn't imagine her mother playing golf. Golf was an outdoor game and her mother was not exactly an outdoorsy kind of person. She didn't like the cold or the rain, and she didn't like getting dirty.

Tess spotted a thicket at the far edge of the golf course. She headed towards it.

"Don't go too far," called her mother. "You might get lost."

"I'll be fine," said Tess.

"I'll show you the pumps, Marjory," said Uncle Randall. "It takes the sewage from the resort and throws it back into the river as clean as a whistle."

Some juncos were sitting on the thimbleberry bushes. Dark-eyed juncos, though she wasn't sure. Grandpa would have known. If he couldn't identify a bird or mushroom or wildflower, he'd search for it in his field guide, then learn it by heart.

Grandpa had a way of naming things.

The nightjar, for instance.

"Those words sit pretty on the tongue," he'd said. "You

can see the night along with the bird." So whenever she saw the flash of white on nightjars' wings as they nose dived at dusk, she pictured "darkness" and remembered the story Grandpa had told her. In ancient times, people called nightjars "goatsuckers" because they believed the birds sucked the milk from goats under cover of darkness. The story wasn't true, but from then on, the birds seemed to possess a kind of magic.

But most of what her grandfather had taught her was practical, like the differences between the huckleberry and the saskatoon, the salal and the blackberry. He'd shown her how to find the butterfly shape in the salmonberry leaf and the furry underside of the thimbleberry. He'd shown her how to harvest the stems of the water parsnip, the bracken, and the water lily, to identify the hazelnut and crabapple trees, to pick Miner's lettuce for salads and wild mint for tea.

Slowly, she had fallen under the spell of the marsh so that now, even in her grandfather's absence, she couldn't turn her back on it.

Suddenly, she felt something hard beneath her feet. It was a golf ball. She picked it up and flung it towards the road. The ball sailed over the spot where the singing tree had once stood. Then it landed in the ditch.

She closed her eyes and, for a moment, she heard hundreds of high-pitched chirps.

But when she looked around her, she saw only the grass and, beyond that, the road. She felt tears spring to her eyes.

The marsh and Grandpa. They were connected somehow, but in a way she couldn't express.

"Tess! What's the matter?"

Her mother was looking at her strangely.

"Nothing," said Tess.

"You look pale."

"I'm fine, Mom. Stop worrying."

"Tell me what's wrong."

"Leave me alone."

Uncle Randall shook his head.

"Tsk. Tsk. You've got to learn how to treat your mother with respect. That's the trouble with young people nowadays. They have no respect for their elders."

Tess walked to the car in silence, wishing she was alone.

On the drive back home, they ran into a rain shower. The rain hit the windshield in sheets. Randall slowed his speed to a crawl, but he kept on talking.

"A group of us are working on the rezoning application. We've asked for a public meeting on July twenty-sixth. Sandhill Resort's applied to expand and the theme park company is waiting in the wings. If Phase B is passed, the rezoning opens a door to the entire development of the polder."

"Dad would have fought it, Randall. You know that."

Randall sighed. "Dad didn't like change."

"That's true. He wanted the polder to stay as it was."

"Marj, Dad's gone," said Randall. "If we can persuade

the mayor and council to approve the rezoning, we'll be free to sell the farm. It will be worth a fortune if we can subdivide it. You could move into town and set up your dressmaking business. You could get out of that drafty old house and buy a new one in a subdivision."

July twenty-sixth! That was only three months away! Three months before the marsh would be destroyed and the cranes would lose their home. And maybe, Willowcreek would be sold, too.

Tess laid her head back on the seat and closed her eyes. It hurt too much to think of it.

So she thought about how warm the summer sun felt on her face, and how delicious the bogberries tasted in August. And when she dozed off, she dreamed that Grandpa was dancing with the cranes.

He was laughing as he danced and the cranes were leaping and bowing. Then suddenly, she saw a long line of bulldozers. The machines were moving slowly across the marsh, mowing down trees and hardhack and filling the sloughs with earth.

Stop! cried Grandpa. But the cranes didn't hear him. The birds wouldn't stop dancing, even after buildings and roads and ferris wheels and hot dogs stands and crowds of people began to magically appear. People were pointing now and shouting.

When Tess woke up, the bulldozers and the buildings and the cranes were gone. Grandpa was gone, too. But she couldn't forget the look on his face.

·5·

Wapato!

Tess hated lunchtime at school. Everyone had a group of friends, except for her. She knew it would take time, but three weeks of standing by herself on the playground was horrible. She imagined everyone was staring at her.

She wished she lived close enough to go home for lunch, but Willowcreek was too far. She was an outsider at school, a city girl who didn't fit in. She began walking across the grass towards the back field, hoping no one would notice her.

In the last two weeks, she'd hardly talked to Zak or Sally. Neither of them had mentioned ghost-hunting again and Tess hadn't brought it up. Zak spent most of his time playing basketball or soccer with the boys. The rest of the time, Rowena and Gail tagged along after him. Sally seemed friendly, but at lunchtime she hung around with her friends from the Katzie Reserve. The Reserve was a small community consisting of a longhouse and a cluster of houses along the water. Tess and Grandpa had gone there once to visit. They'd watched the Katzie returning from salmon fishing.

Tess spotted some girls from her class sitting in the baseball dugout near the ball field and thought of walking over to them. But what would she say?

Hi, do you mind if I join you? Or *what are you doing?* Or maybe she should just say *hi* and hope they'd invite her to join them.

But what if they didn't? What if they just stared at her? She couldn't imagine anything worse.

She walked slowly in the direction of the dugout. The closer she got the more queasy her stomach felt.

Hi, do you always hang out here?

Nothing sounded right. But maybe it wasn't the words, exactly, but how she said them. If her voice shook, that would be embarrassing. That's what happened when she had to do a speech at school last year. If she could say the words without thinking about them, then they seemed to come out better. Tess noticed Rowena always had a bunch of friends around her, but she never seemed to think for a second about what to say.

Tess heard laughter coming from the dugout. No. She couldn't do it. Quickly, she turned and headed towards a wooded area at the far end of the school grounds. There were alders and a blackberry thicket growing against the fence and, on the other side, there was a slough.

Nearing the back fence, she heard a loud rattling call. *Rat-a-tat-rat-a-tat.* Kingfisher. It was one of the first calls Grandpa had taught her.

Finally, she located the bird. It was sitting on an alder branch above her. She watched the bird for awhile, then took out her bird notebook and began to write.

May 5, 12:20 p.m. Meadowland Elementary

I saw a kingfisher today. It was near the slough in the back field of the school yard. It's a blue-grey bird with a large crest on its head. Its head looks too big for its body. The kingfisher flew over the fence to the water. It beat its wings quickly, hovering over the surface, then dove head first with a splash. When the bird came up, a tiny fish was hanging out of its beak. Then it flew back to the tree and swallowed the fish in one gulp.

"What are you doing?" asked a voice from behind her. Tess jumped.

Rowena and Gail had followed her.

"Writing in my bird notebook. The kingfisher up there just caught a fish."

"Where?" asked Rowena.

"Up there," said Tess pointing.

"Oh, I see it," said Rowena.

"Here, kingfisher! Here boy!" said Gail, waving to the bird. The kingfisher let out a loud rattle, then flew off.

"It's not a dog, Gail," scowled Rowena. "It's a bird."

Rowena turned to Tess. "So I hear you like birds."

"Yes ... I guess so," said Tess.

"What's your favourite then?"

"My favourite?"

"Bird," said Rowena impatiently, "your favourite bird."

"Cranes," said Tess.

Rowena nodded. "I've seen lots of cranes."

"Me, too," piped in Gail. "I saw one today on the way to school."

Tess knew that couldn't be true. Cranes were shy and secretive. They avoided people. There were too few of them to be seen that often.

"You probably saw herons," said Tess. "Herons and cranes look alike. Lots of people get them mixed up. In the air, a heron's neck looks crooked, but a crane's looks straight ... oh, and cranes have a red crest on their head."

Rowena yawned. "Whatever," she said.

Tess felt her cheeks grow warm. She should have kept quiet. Let them think they'd seen a million cranes! Why should she care?

Rowena nudged Gail, "Here comes Zak. Sally's with him."

"Rowena!" shouted Zak. "Do you and Gail want to play basketball? Rob's saving the court."

"Sure!" said Rowena. "Come on, Gailsie."

Sally waved. "Hi, Tess!"

"Done any ghost-hunting lately?" asked Zak.

"No," said Tess.

"I still want to go," said Zak.

Rowena stared at Zak, her eyes narrowing.

"You can come, too, Row," he added.

"I don't believe in ghosts," said Rowena curtly. "I thought you wanted to play basketball."

"Be there in a minute," said Zak. "Why don't we go on Saturday, Tess?"

"Huh ... sure ... okay," said Tess.

Rowena glared at Zak, then stomped off. Gail followed her.

"Wait up!" cried Zak, chasing them across the field. Then suddenly he turned back to Tess and shouted, "I'll phone you."

"*What* does he see in Rowena?" asked Sally.

Tess shrugged. "She's pretty."

"The other kids are scared of her."

Tess watched Zak catch up to Rowena. They were standing by the swings talking. Then Rowena and Zak walked to the basketball court, arm in arm.

Tess noticed that Zak didn't ask *her* to play basketball. Not that she wanted to. She'd never played sports — except during gym periods at school. Her mom was always afraid she'd get hurt. But she wasn't good at sports anyway. Not like Martine. Martine played soccer and baseball and she took skating lessons twice a week. Martine loved skating as much as Tess loved birding.

"She doesn't like me," said Tess to Sally.

"Who?"

"Rowena."

"She's jealous."

"Of what?" asked Tess, puzzled. "She has all the friends."

"Maybe because you have nice clothes and you're from the city. And because Zak seems to like you."

"Zak likes everyone."

Sally laughed. "That's true."

There was a long silence. Tess wished she could talk about nothing, the way Rowena did. It came in handy during long awkward moments like this.

"What were you and Rowena looking at?" asked Sally.

"A kingfisher," said Tess, "but it flew away."

"Too bad I missed it," said Sally. "The kingfisher's a good luck bird for fishermen. My grandfather says if you see one you'll be able to catch fish as easy as holding out your hand. Do you like fishing?"

"I've never gone. Do you?"

"Yup. My dad and my grandfather make their living by fishing. Once when I went out with them, I caught a salmon as long as my arm."

"Fishing sounds like fun."

"It is. Maybe you could come with us one day." Sally picked a piece of grass and began to chew on it. "It's nice here. Quiet. It's a good place to get away from people."

Tess nodded. "My favourite place is a sandbar at the end of Widgeon Creek. It's really pretty there and it's perfectly quiet except for the birds. My grandfather and I canoed there last summer."

"I know the place. But it won't be quiet much longer," said Sally, "not once they finish that golf resort."

"Sandhill?"

Sally picked up a twig and threw it into the bushes.

"Yes. My grandfather turns his head whenever he passes that place. He says that land is sacred to the Katzie. It's where Swaneset, the Katzie chief and supernatural being, did his great deeds."

"What did he do?" asked Tess.

"He made all the sloughs and the hills around here. See that hill?"

"Sheridan Hill?"

"Yeah. The Katzie say that Sheridan Hill used to be a huge mountain. It used to be so tall our people used to climb it so they could reach the sky. Swaneset didn't think that people should do that, so he took five or six huge stones and threw them at that mountain. The stones broke the top off the mountain and that's how the hills around here were made. So the Katzie could no longer reach the sky."

Sally picked up a stick and she began to draw in the mud.

"Then Swaneset drew lines all over his face. Like this. He began praying to The Lord Above and the wiggly lines became sloughs. That was good because then the Katzie could gather Indian potato and wild cranberries and lots of other foods. Swaneset also brought the eulechon and the salmon to our people. Then he married the crane sisters but he left them after awhile, because he didn't like how they got their food from the mud."

"Who were the crane sisters?"

"A long long time ago they were human, but later Khaals changed them into birds."

"Who was Khaals?"

Sally thought for awhile before answering. "My grandfather calls him the Transformer because he changed people into different things, like animals or rocks or birds or even the winds. But he was also a trickster. Because the crane sisters danced and dug in the mud for their food, Khaals changed them into birds who spent their days doing that."

Tess glanced up at Sheridan Hill. Somehow the hill looked different to her now.

"I like your stories," said Tess.

"My grandfather always tells me stories," said Sally. "He says when he's gone, I have to tell them to others."

"My grandfather told me stories, too. They were usually about birds."

They skirted the fence as they talked.

"Why did the crane sisters dig for their food? What did they eat?" asked Tess.

"*Wapato*. Indian potato."

"Is that story true?" asked Tess.

Sally shrugged. "Some people say it's a myth. Others believe it's true. But *wapato* is real. My grandmother used to gather it from the sloughs. She'd wade into the water and pull the roots up with her toes. The roots taste good."

"What's it look like?"

"The leaves are shaped like an arrow," said Sally. "There's probably some growing in the slough over there."

"I'd love to see it!" said Tess.

This was the kind of adventure her grandfather would have loved — searching for an interesting plant or rare bird.

"It's off the school property," said Sally, "... if we get caught ..."

But Tess saw the mischievous look in Sally's eyes.

"Come on," said Tess.

Checking to see if the coast was clear, they quickly climbed over the fence.

"Once we're on the other side," said Sally, "they won't be able to see us."

The slough was still. Clouds and mountains and trees were reflected on its surface, except for the shoreline which was covered with pond lily.

"There's some *wapato*," said Sally. "Over there by that rock. We'll have to wade out for it."

Tess looked at her city shoes. They were covered with mud. She kicked them off. Sally took hers off, too, and rolled up her jeans. Tess hoisted up her jumper and they waded in. The water was cold and stagnant and mucky. A corner of the hem of her woolen jumper began to soak up slough water. Why had she worn her city clothes? They weren't meant for walking through fields or wading through sloughs.

Tess checked off a list inside her head of every slimy thing she could imagine: frogs' eggs, duckweed, salamanders, pond lily, crayfish, blood suckers — then prayed she wouldn't step on them. She loved nature, but there was a limit.

The *wapato* leaves were floating on the surface. She couldn't wait to look up the plant in her grandfather's field guide. *Wapato*, the crane sisters' favourite food. Like most plants, it probably had several names.

"We could pick it with our hands," said Sally shivering, "but we'd probably get our clothes even more wet and muddy. Or we could do it the Indian way — with our toes. Like this."

Sally wound her toes around the stalk of the plant and began to pull. Tess tried to copy her, holding up her jumper above her knees.

"The stalk's slippery," said Tess.

"Grab it with your big toe. Then pull really hard."

"I'm trying," said Tess with a giggle.

"Got one!" said Sally holding her leg up with the root dangling between her toes. Then she lost her balance and one leg slid between Tess's legs and both of them fell backwards into the slime.

"*Wapato*," said Sally, handing Tess the root.

"Neat!" said Tess, beginning to shiver.

"Let's get out of here," said Sally. "The water is freezing."

Tess started to laugh. "Look at you," she said, pointing.

"You should talk!" said Sally, trying to brush the mud off her jeans between fits of giggles.

Tess's clothes were covered with thick brown sludge from her waist to her toes. The mud felt like slug slime and smelled of slough. As she climbed out, the water around her turned a deep rusty brown.

Tess examined her prize. "It looks more like an onion than a potato." Her hands were shaking from the cold.

"It's harvested in the fall," said Sally. "The root is bigger then."

"There they are!" yelled a high-pitched voice from the opposite side of the fence. Rowena.

A teacher, surrounded by a group of kids, was staring at them from the other side of the fence.

"You two!" yelled the teacher. "You're out of bounds! Get over here immediately!"

Rowena was standing beside the teacher. She had a smirk on her face.

"What are we going to tell them?" Tess whispered as she hugged herself to keep warm.

"*Wapato*. We'll tell them we were gathering *wapato*," said Sally.

"*Wapato?*" asked Tess's mother over dinner that evening.

"What in the world's *wapato?*" asked Randall. His voice was booming. Whenever he spoke, Tess had an urge to turn a switch like turning down the volume of a radio. Everything about Uncle Randall was big. He was tall — six-foot-four — and broad. And when he walked the floors of the farmhouse made a loud creak.

Wild potato. Swamp potato. Duck potato. Swan potato. Arrowhead.

"Well?" he asked.

"It's ... a ... kind of plant," said Tess. She felt stupid, unable to explain.

Her uncle gave her a look of disbelief.

Her mother was pacing up and down the kitchen floor.

"I was really upset when I got the phone call from the principal. You could have drowned. I've told you time and time again to stay away from the sloughs! They're dangerous!"

"The water wasn't deep," replied Tess, weakly.

Marjory rubbed her forehead, as she did when a headache was coming on.

"You could have been suspended, too. That girl Sally should have known about not leaving the school grounds at lunchtime."

"It wasn't her fault," said Tess. "I knew the rules, too."

"Why did you break them, then?" asked her mom.

"I don't know," said Tess. And it was true. She didn't know why she'd done it.

"I hope you will both excuse me," said Randall stiffly. "I am expected at a meeting." He grabbed a pile of pamphlets and stuffed them into his briefcase with a loud snap. Tess saw the word "Sandhill" in bold red print.

"You should be ashamed of yourself, young lady, causing your mother so much worry. I hope you will learn something from your week of detentions." Randall glanced in the mirror. He tried to brush down his hair, but it still stuck out in a million places. He took a black felt hat from a box in the hall closet, placed it on his head, buttoned up his long black overcoat and walked out the door.

· 6 ·

Unexpected Events

TESS DIDN'T MIND the week of detentions. She and Sally had to sit outside the principal's office every day for an hour. It was boring, but the long walk home together was fun. It gave them time to get to know each other. And Sally made her laugh.

After a couple of days, they began to eat lunch together. And by the time they'd served their last detention on Friday afternoon, Tess felt as though she were losing a friend.

"I'm nervous about tomorrow morning," said Tess.

"Ghost-hunting would make anyone nervous," said Sally.

Tess laughed. "It's meeting Zak I'm nervous about! I hardly know him."

"Zak wouldn't hurt a flea."

"Would you come with us?" begged Tess. "Just this once — to keep me company?"

"You don't know what you're asking," said Sally. "I'm scared of ghosts a lot more than you're scared of Zak."

"Please?" said Tess.

"Okay, city girl. I'll go."

Tess hugged her. "Yes! I'll meet you an hour before sunrise."

"What time's that?"

"Four o'clock," said Tess sheepishly.

Sally groaned. "Four o'clock? Ugh! I hate early mornings. Except when I go fishing."

"We'll go fishing for a ghost," said Tess.

"I just hope we don't catch one," replied Sally.

Tess woke to the sound of her alarm clock at three-forty-five Saturday morning. That meant she had barely ten minutes to get dressed and out the door. The Katzie story of the ghost weighed on her mind. Zak had protested against meeting at three. Four o'clock was early enough, he'd said. Secretly, Tess felt relieved.

Now every time she heard an owl she thought of the polder ghost. But maybe the polder ghost was a protector, reminding people not to harm its territory. Maybe spirits had territories, just as animals did.

Her bedroom was dark and cold and when she opened the window and stuck her hand outside, she felt a fine rain on her skin. Rain again! It was hard to get used to. Spring weather on the West Coast was wetter than the weather back East. And the Pitt Polder was one of the wettest places in the lower mainland.

She dressed quickly and, still half asleep, stumbled outside. As she walked through the field, she could hear the bull frogs and leopard frogs singing to their mates.

Go around, go around, sang the bull frogs.

Too deep, too deep, chimed in the leopard frogs. Their mates were silent. They were too busy laying eggs along the shallows of the sloughs to sing.

Clouds drifted dreamily across a crescent moon. Between the moon and the mountains, a pair of barn owls glided silently above the bog.

A coyote began to howl. Tess froze, trying to pinpoint the animal's location. She figured the coyote was about a quarter mile away. What if she met the animal on the path? She shivered with fear. She wanted to run back to the house. But Sally would never forgive her if she didn't show up.

I'm not afraid. I'm not afraid. I'm not afraid.

Grandpa told her that animals could sense if someone was afraid. They could smell fear. She quickened her stride and walked steadily until she saw Sally and Zak ahead of her on the dyke. Then she broke into a run.

"What's wrong?" asked Sally.

"Coyote! Did you hear it?" asked Tess breathing hard.

"I heard it," said Sally shivering.

"There's three of us," said Zak. "It won't hurt us."

Zak was probably right. Grandpa hadn't been afraid of coyotes. Why should she?

They began walking along the dyke road, looking for signs of movement. They took turns scanning the marsh with Tess's binoculars, but they saw nothing that resembled a ghost. As they walked, they talked in whispers.

"My mom told me about your grandfather dying," said Zak.

Tess didn't reply.

"Is that why you and your mom decided to move here?" asked Zak.

"I suppose so," said Tess. "My uncle needed help with the blueberry harvest. He never liked farming, though. He'd rather sell real estate."

"Your grandfather was a good blueberry farmer," said Zak, quickly. "That's what my mom said."

"Yes," said Tess. "He didn't use pesticides, even though it was harder. He didn't want to harm the birds."

They walked until they came to a slough ditch filled with water. "That's where I saw the figure," said Tess. "In the far field."

Zak jumped over the ditch first.

"Careful, Sally. The water's deep," he said. Then he held out his hand and Sally jumped across.

Her mother's warnings flashed into Tess's head. *Stay away from the slough.*

But that was impossible. Sloughs ran through the polder like veins on a leaf.

"Your turn, city girl," said Zak.

Tess drew a deep breath and jumped across the ditch. Zak caught her hand and pulled her up onto the bank.

"Thanks," she said. Her hand was shaking.

She wondered if that meant she liked him. In the past, as soon as she liked a boy, she got nervous. She hated that. It spoiled all the fun.

They walked through the marsh, until they came to a windfall log under a row of cottonwood trees. The log was hidden in shadows, so it made a good viewing spot. They sat on the log and ate the gingersnaps Tess had stuffed into her raincoat pocket. They were soft, but they still tasted good.

Tess felt Zak's eyes on her.

"Where's your dad?" he asked.

Tess was taken aback. Zak was always asking questions. Personal questions.

"He's dead."

Zak's face fell. "Oh. I'm sorry."

"It's okay. He died when I was really young. In a plane crash. I don't remember him. What about your dad?"

"He doesn't live with us anymore. My mom and dad separated last year. Then he moved to Alberta." Zak's eyes softened. "I've only seen him twice since he left."

"Oh." She didn't know what to say. What was worse? Never knowing a dad or growing up with one, then having him move far away?

"I'd miss my dad if he left," said Sally.

"Sometimes, I miss mine," said Zak. "But my parents were always fighting." He grabbed a stick and began hitting the log. "At least it's quiet at home now."

I'm not the only one who's having a hard time. Zak just hides it better.

"My house is never quiet," said Sally. "I have three brothers and a baby sister and my grandmother and grandfather live downstairs. Then there's my dad's fishermen friends and the smokehouse people who come and visit grandfather."

"Who are the smokehouse people?" asked Tess.

"You know that big grey building on the reserve?"

Tess nodded.

"That's the smokehouse," said Sally. "It's like a church. My grandfather spends a lot of time down there. If someone's spirit is sick, he heals it. Or if they have something wrong with them, like headaches or a sore that won't go away, he can make them better."

A hollow musical hum filled the air — then a cry.

"What's that?" asked Sally anxiously.

"Nighthawk," said Tess. "That sound is the air rushing through the bird's feathers as it dives through the air. It's hunting for insects."

"Whew," said Sally. "I thought it was a ghost."

After watching for awhile, they returned to the dyke road. The mist had grown thicker, veiling the polder in a thick grey shroud. They could see no more than a metre or two ahead of them.

Suddenly, they heard a loud snap. Something was moving through the bushes on the slough side.

"Let's get off the road!" said Zak.

They scrambled down the dyke ditch and crouched in the marsh grass. They sat there in silence for a long time

Tess could see a faint glimmer of light on the horizon.

"Look!" said Tess. "Over there. On that sandbar island."

"What is it?" whispered Sally.

"I don't know. But it's as tall as the hardhack bushes."

"Maybe it's the ghost," said Zak.

They heard rustling then footsteps.

"It's coming this way!" said Zak.

Suddenly they heard a loud trumpeting and a flutter.

Zak's mouth flew open.

"A crane!" said Tess.

The crane was about forty metres away. Trembling with excitement, Tess slowly turned the focus on her binoculars. The bird came into startling clarity.

There was the greenish black of the crane's eyes, the bare red cap of the forehead and crown, the long slender grey legs.

"Look," she said, handing the glasses to Zak.

"Wow!" said Zak. "It's huge. Wait a minute. Its feathers look red! I thought the cranes were a pale grey."

"They are," said Tess, "but when they're old enough to take a mate, they use their beaks to paint their feathers with mud. The iron in the mud rusts and the rust stains the feathers a reddish brown. Each crane pair has the same markings."

"Let me see," said Sally.

They watched the crane rooting in the mud as the marmalade sun rose slowly between the Golden Ears Mountains. With the dawn, the mood of the polder changed. The slough became a moving picture of liquid light with the clouds and mountains and sky reflected on its surface.

A breeze sprang up and the cottonwoods began their soft whispery singing. On the dyke road, a band of swallows performed acrobatics.

"Hey, I think the crane is standing over a nest," said Sally. "It looks like a messy one. Yes ... it's sitting on it now." She handed Tess the binoculars.

Sally was right. It *was* a nest!

"A nest means babies," said Tess.

"Aw," said Sally.

"If only Grandpa could be here," said Tess. "He would be so happy."

"Maybe he is," said Sally, putting her arm around Tess's shoulder.

"Yeah!" said Zak. "Maybe he's your guardian angel. My mom believes her Aunt Sandra is her guardian angel. She died when my mom was ten."

"Do you think it's possible?" asked Tess, hopefully.

"For sure," said Sally.

"It's possible," said Zak.

Suddenly, a loud thump broke the silence. Then the sound of footsteps behind them.

Tess started.

"What's that?" she asked, shining her flashlight into the thicket.

"Probably a bird or a mouse," said Zak.

"Maybe a coyote," whispered Tess.

The sound was louder now. A scraping kind of sound. Something or someone was coming their way. It wasn't a crane. Tess was sure of that. She huddled against Sally.

"It sounds creepy," said Sally.

Tess could feel goose bumps forming on her arms and legs.

More footsteps. Closer than before.

"Who is it?" asked Zak in a high thin voice.

The footsteps stopped.

"Let's get out of here," said Zak.

"I thought you wanted to solve the mystery," whispered Tess.

"Next time," said Zak.

"You'll regret it if you chicken out," said Tess, trying to sound brave.

Zak gave her an indignant look.

"Come on, then," he said. He took the flashlight from Sally and inched his way towards the noise. Tess and Sally followed closely behind him.

Sally pulled on Zak's jacket.

"Listen," she said.

A twig broke. Someone was coming towards them.

Zak reared back. Then he began to run.

Tess took Sally's hand and followed him.

"Look!" gasped Tess.

They stopped, too surprised to speak.

·7·

The Bird Woman

A TINY WOMAN with snow white hair stood before them. She was wearing a long raincoat with a hood. It was covered with pockets and zippers. A pair of binoculars hung around her neck and she carried a spotting scope in one hand.

Birder.

"Hello," chirped the woman.

She looked like a grandmother with her startlingly white hair and soft voice. But there was something about her that seemed young, perhaps the small quick movements of her head and hands. Then Tess noticed the woman was wearing a hood.

"Where did you come from?" asked Zak.

"From the road."

Tess and Sally exchanged looks.

"I'm Clara Williams."

"The bird woman!" said Zak.

"Zak!" said Tess.

Clara chuckled. "Don't bother me a bit, dear. I've been called that for about fifty years."

"I'm Zak. This is Tess ..."

"De Boer?" asked the woman.

Tess nodded. The bird woman shook their hands warmly.

How did the woman know her last name? Then she remembered that people knew their neighbours in the country.

"Were you kids ghost-hunting?" asked Clara.

Tess nodded.

"Thought so," said the bird woman. "Oh my, that brings back memories. When we were kids, we *loved* to go ghost-hunting. That polder ghost has been haunting these parts for a long long time."

Sally gave Tess a questioning look.

"My parents used to go ghost-hunting, too," said Zak. "And my grandparents."

"Oh, we all did," said Clara. "And there's a few old timers around who say they saw it. They say they were never the same again." Clara glanced quickly at her watch. "Oh, oh, the crane concert's about to begin. Did you see the crane hen?"

"Yes," said Tess, "and the nest, too!"

Clara put her hand on her heart. "Yes. It's so exciting, isn't it? If you want seats, you'll have to hurry."

Sally frowned. "Where are we going?"

"To my blind, of course," said the bird woman. "It's not too fancy, just a bunch of alder branches and mud tied together with some rope and a couple of stakes. But it's a perfect hiding place to watch the cranes on the nest, if you're quiet."

Zak was already at the bird woman's heels, but Sally held back. She looked worried.

"She's harmless," urged Tess. "It'll be fun."

"As much fun as gathering *wapato*?" asked Sally, dryly.

"More," said Tess.

"Then we're *really* in trouble," said Sally. They both giggled.

The bird woman bobbed through the wet grass so quickly Tess could barely keep up. The blind was located on a sandbar along a bend in the slough. The bird woman had piled the branches about two metres high in a U-shape. It formed a small enclosure just big enough to hide the four of them if they huddled together.

Clara removed a large rubber sheet from a small pack she'd slung on her back and spread it on the ground. She adjusted the folding legs of her spotting scope, then pushed the scope through an opening in the branches of the blind.

The bird woman began to pull small branches from the front of the blind, so they could look out.

"There you go," whispered Clara. "Front row seats."

Tess peered out the opening. It was a perfect spot to see the crane nest.

"Come and look," she said, motioning to Sally and Zak.

The air was chilly, but Tess felt warm inside. She liked Sally almost as much as Martine. Zak was nice too, though she couldn't understand why he liked Rowena.

Clara removed her stop watch from her wrist, took out a notebook and pencil from the pocket of her raincoat, and laid the items in front of her.

"Ready," she said with a sigh.

"What's that?" asked Zak.

"My bird notes," said Clara. "I keep track of things in my field notebook. I record the dates and times of my sightings and the length and duration of the cranes' calls."

"I keep bird notes, too," said Tess, shyly.

"You do?"

"Yes," said Tess, "ever since I was five years old."

Clara smiled. "Why that's wonderful!"

Tess reddened under the bird woman's gaze. "May I have a look at your field notebook?" she asked.

"Of course," said Clara, handing her the book.

Tess skimmed through the small notebook, chose a page at random and began to read. Sally and Zak peered over her shoulder.

March 30. Field south of Cod Island, Pitt Polder

2:00 a.m. – I entered the blind. No rain. I crawled into my sleeping bag and slept for a couple hours.

4:00 a.m. – Temperature: 18 degrees centigrade. Cranes have been quiet lately, trying to avoid attracting attention to the nest. A good sign. Hopefully, the cranes are incubating their eggs.

4:20 a.m. – Saw the male fly in from the north. The crane landed a few metres from the nest. A few seconds later, I heard the unison call. 75 seconds duration.

4:24 a.m. – A neighbouring pair answered the first unison call. Approximately three kilometres away, near the junction of the Alouette River.

4:30 a.m. – Heard a faint call from the southwest. Near the bog.

4:38 a.m. – First solo call this morning. It's probably the bachelor crane I spotted near Blaney Bog last week. Call repeated 3 times at 40 second intervals.

5:03 a.m. – Sunrise. Sky clear. Two more cranes called from the northeast. One of the cranes called 8 times without interruption.

5:17 a.m. – An American bittern flushed from some nearby sweet gale bushes. Eastern sky is beginning to cloud over towards the mountains.

5:24 a.m. – A flock of mallards swimming up the slough.

5:21 a.m. – Four cranes flew over the blind. They looked like they were playing. They were climbing, diving, twisting, side-slipping. The birds higher up changed places with the others flying below them. The cranes were flapping their wings in unison, then they flew off towards Widgeon Creek. As of the above date,

there are only 20 cranes in the entire polder. 8 mated
pairs and 4 juveniles. 4 less cranes than last year. Every
year the flock is dwindling.
Clara out.

Sally turned to Clara. "What do you do with all the information?"

"Share it with other birders, of course. There are some birders in Wisconsin and a few fellows in the ministry of environment I keep in touch with. But mostly I do it for me ... and the cranes, of course."

Kneeling in front of the scope, the bird woman adjusted the focus.

"There she is! Oh, she's a beauty," whispered Clara, guiding Tess gently towards the scope.

Tess handed Zak her binoculars. She pressed her eye against the small round glass of the spotting scope.

The hen crane was sitting on the nest. She could see the long slender bill, the dark round staring eyes, the pale mouse-grey feathers.

"Oh!" said Tess in amazement. She'd forgotten how much larger things looked through a spotting scope.

Suddenly from the distance, Tess heard the first call.

"Unison call," said Clara, taking out her stopwatch. She pressed the timer, her forehead wrinkled, one ear cocked to one side. "Forty second duration. Directly west. Near Blaney Bog."

Tess remembered seeing the same look of intense concentration on Grandpa's face as he timed the calls with his pocket watch. He'd press the silver knob on top to start the timer. Then he'd record the information in his notebook.

Tess thought it was probably that attention to detail which separated the casual birder from birders like Grandpa or Clara. And she wanted to be as fine a birder as Grandpa had been. She decided that when she got home she would look for her grandfather's pocket watch. She'd learn to time the calls, too.

"Listen!" said Sally. "Do you hear it?"

"Yes," said Tess. "The call's coming from the northwest."

"Yes," said Clara. "From the Maple Ridge polder. Cod Island, I'd say. Good morning, Cod Island cranes!"

Tess tried to distinguish the higher voice of the female from the lower of the male. Though the calls of the pair were different in rhythm — the female gave two quick calls for every single call of the male — the calls fit together so perfectly that the duet sounded like a solo.

The unison songs were comforting to Tess. She imagined the cranes calling to their mates, announcing their arrival home.

Home. The cranes had a home. Where is mine? Toronto? Willowcreek? Neither one? Maybe home was more than a place. Maybe it meant friends. People who cared about you.

Tess stared into the darkness. The marsh was silent now. No one spoke for a long time.

"Intermission," said Clara, as she tucked her notebook into her pocket.

"How can you tell exactly how many cranes there are?" asked Zak.

"I've been tracking the flock since late March," said Clara. "By listening to the loudness and direction of the unison calls I can determine the location of each nesting pair. Then I add the solo calls of the bachelor cranes."

"The Katzie say there used to be thousands of cranes here," said Sally.

"Used to be," said Clara sadly.

"Where did they all go?" asked Tess.

"The way of the eulechon, the sturgeon, and the seals," said Clara. "The large numbers disappeared with development. But people didn't realize how important wetlands were then. They were called wastelands. The cranes suffered most. Your grandfather was acutely aware of that."

"You knew my grandfather?"

Clara started. "We went to school together."

"Really!"

"Nothing unusual about that," said Clara abruptly.

There was something in Clara's reply that made Tess curious. But the bird woman turned away quickly. She took out a crumpled up cotton hat from her pocket and pulled it down over her face. Minutes later, she was fast asleep.

Sally whispered to Tess. "You can lean against me, if you want."

Tess placed her head against Sally's shoulder.

"What about me?" said Zak, in a teasing voice. He looked at Tess.

"Sure," said Tess. Her heart raced at the thought. Zak placed his head on her shoulder, yawned and closed his eyes.

Tess suddenly thought of her grandfather. She thought of those warm summer nights when they'd sat together in the darkness waiting for the song of the sandhills. But she pushed these thoughts aside. She was afraid she might cry. Whenever she felt like this, she'd keep herself busy. This morning there was nothing to do but wait.

· 8 ·

More About Cranes

A LOUD BUGLING *hurr-roo-oo-roo-roo* sounded in the distance.

"Crane!" said Clara. She pushed back the brim of her hat and set her stop watch. She was mumbling under her breath and flapping her hands around.

"Now where is my notebook? Oh, there. Okay, I'm ready. It's not too far away. Time? Five-thirty a.m. Good. Good. Things are looking up."

Tess shook herself awake. Sally's head was still on her shoulder.

"Sally," she whispered. Sally woke with a start, then stretched. Zak was sitting up. His eyes were half closed.

Tess peered out the opening of the blind.

"I see it," she whispered. Even from a distance, she recognized the quick upstroke of the crane's flight.

The bird gradually slowed its flight, then began to circle the nest. Suddenly he lowered his long slender legs, spread out his wings, and began gliding slowly downward. The crane looked strange and funny, like a bird clown hanging onto a parachute. He landed on the sandbar with a skid.

"That crane looks so tall," said Zak.

"He's a greater sandhill," whispered Clara. "They stand about four feet. The greaters are a subspecies. The lesser sandhills are smaller and more common."

Once on the ground, the crane flapped his wings three times and bowed with a grand flourish. Then he began to serenade his mate. The smaller crane stood up and greeted him with a high musical rattle, the two songs blending into one.

When the unison song ended, the hen crane took small halting steps, lifting each leg high in the air behind herself.

"What's she doing?" asked Tess.

"Being cautious," said Clara. "When she or her mate changes places on the nest, they do everything to avoid pushing the eggs out."

Once safely off the nest, the hen flapped her wings and bowed to her partner, then wandered over to a clump of sedges and began to root.

The male strutted round and round the nest, his head moving quickly forward with each step. Every so often, he paused to preen his feathers. Finally, he straddled the nest and began to rearrange and shift straying strands of marsh grass and sedge, using the tip of his bill.

He's tidying the nest.

His housework complete, the crane turned the eggs with his bill and sat on them.

As if taking her cue, the hen took several running steps and sprang into the air.

Tess watched her until she disappeared into the trees.

"They've just changed guard," said Tess.

"What's that mean?" asked Zak.

"They're taking turns sitting on the eggs," said Tess.

"How many eggs do they lay?" asked Sally.

"Two usually, but sometimes three," said Clara. "When food is plentiful, both chicks will survive. Each parent takes care of one chick. But in the polder, usually only one chick will survive. The strongest will drive the weakest away."

Tess swallowed. "How does the chick die?"

"Drowning or starvation," replied Clara.

Clara patted Tess's hand. "Sometimes, though, a chick will survive *without* parents. It's unusual, but it does happen."

"The parents should protect them," said Sally.

"They try," said Clara, "but it happens in spite of them. Mother Nature has to look at the big picture. Sometimes the chance of a single chick surviving is better than two."

"But if there are only twenty cranes in the polder flock, are they in danger of extinction?" asked Zak.

"Of course they are!" cried Clara. "Cranes are sensitive creatures. They can't tolerate human intrusion. And right now, there's a proposal up before the mayor and council to change the zoning that would allow more development!"

"That's terrible," said Sally.

"Worse than terrible. It's disastrous! I've been fretting, not sleeping, hardly eating. The municipal council will make their decision on July 26! I had been dreaming about it for weeks. Until one night, I woke up in the middle of the night and I said to myself, 'Clara, no use driving yourself crazy. What can you DO to save the cranes?' Emphasis on the DO. So I started making plans. And as soon as I made my plans I felt better. Then I went to bed and slept sounder than I'd slept in months."

Then the old woman pulled out a thermos from her backpack. She smiled sweetly.

"Tea anyone?" she asked, passing a plastic cup around.

"It's wild mint, picked in the meadow."

"My grandfather used to make me that kind!" said Tess.

Clara raised one eyebrow, but she made no comment, merely handed Tess the cup.

Tess sipped the tea. It smelled like field flowers — fragrant, with a sweet taste. She remembered how it warmed her throat and how comforting it was to sip a hot drink in the early morning light. She remembered her grandfather's hands — how brown and wrinkled they were, but soft. His eyes were soft in a different way.

There were so many things she wished she'd told him. I love you, for instance. He'd never said it either, but he didn't need to. She knew he loved her.

And they had so much in common.

Not like she and her mother. They seemed opposite in every way. Tess loved the outdoors. Mom was happiest sitting inside, making beautiful things from cloth. But Mom couldn't see how beautiful nature could be. Neither could Tess, until she met Grandpa. With Grandpa, she discovered an important part of herself.

"So what are you going to DO?" asked Zak.

"DO?" asked the bird woman.

"To save the cranes!"

"Oh dear, I forgot to tell you, didn't I," said Clara chuckling. "Well, first I plan to take a crane egg from several nests around here. Then I'm going to incubate the eggs. And finally — I'm keeping my toes and fingers crossed — I plan to release the young cranes."

Tess felt a catch in her throat.

"You're going to *steal* the cranes' eggs?" asked Tess.

"It's a drastic measure," said the bird woman, suddenly serious. "But with so few cranes left I have to do something."

Tess felt unsettled. Grandpa wouldn't even pick a wildflower. He'd never steal a crane egg.

"But are you ... allowed?" asked Tess.

"You mean do I have permission from the ministry of environment?"

Tess shrugged. "I guess so," she said. She wasn't sure who you had to ask about such things.

"Yes. They've given me the go-ahead. They don't have the funding to do it themselves, so they're grateful for the help. If the numbers weren't so low, I wouldn't consider it. But the polder is the only nesting area in the lower mainland, except for the one or two pair in Burn's Bog. But even one more chick could mean the difference between the survival of the species around here."

One chick. Did you know it was that bad, Grandpa? But you must have. You knew where all the cranes nested.

"Could we help?" asked Zak, glancing at Tess and Sally.

"Yes, could we?" echoed Sally.

"Heavens, no," said the bird woman shaking her head, "though the sentiment's appreciated. Your parents wouldn't thank me for that! Not on your life! Cranes have powerful legs and dagger-like bills. They're not like kittens!" Then she shook with laughter. "Now don't look so disappointed. You could all help me set up the incubators."

"When?" asked Zak.

"Next week if everything goes well," said Clara.

Tess still had doubts.

She stared at Clara's features, searching for a sign. The bird woman's rosy cheeks and large huckleberry blue eyes and wide grin seemed out of place on such a small face. Her face was so changeable, she could look like a girl one minute and an old lady the next. And nothing she wore matched. Not the purple and pink silk scarf with her camouflage green jacket. Not even her socks peeking over her hiking boots. One was grey and the other was brown.

All at once Tess smiled to herself. She'd finally figured out Clara's bird. Barn owl!

"Features?" Grandpa would have asked.

Easy! Both had heart-shaped faces. The barn owl had white feathers. Clara had white hair and pale skin. And they're both pretty.

Tess, you are an ornithological genius!

That's probably what Grandpa would have said to her.

For a moment Tess's eyes met Clara's. If the bird woman was successful in raising the cranes and increasing the crane population, wouldn't Grandpa have approved? She'd seen the look on Clara's face when she talked about the cranes. The old woman loved the cranes as much as Grandpa had.

"I'll help, too," said Tess.

"It's settled then," said the bird woman. "And I'll have a surprise for you when you pay me a visit."

"What is it?" asked Tess.

"If I told you ..."

"... it wouldn't be a surprise," said Tess and Sally in unison.

๑

After leaving Clara that morning, Tess glanced at her watch and yawned. It was almost seven o'clock and she'd been up since four. She climbed the stairs like a sleepwalker.

The house was so quiet she could hear the clock ticking in the dining room. Her mother and Uncle Randall must still be sleeping. They were both night owls and liked to sleep in on weekends.

Tess crawled under her bed covers with her clothes on and slept until noon.

"Are you sick?" asked Marjory, when Tess entered the kitchen yawning. Her mother had yards of white satin covering the table and chairs.

"Just tired," said Tess, which wasn't *exactly* a lie.

"What are you working on?" asked Tess.

"A wedding gown," said her mother. "It has sequins on the bodice, so it's going to take a few weeks to finish."

"Sequins! Ugh! I don't know how you do it," said Tess shaking her head. Once she'd sewn hundreds of sequins on a dress to help her mother out. It had taken days. At the time, she'd decided that sewing shiny little circles on a piece of cloth was the most frustrating activity in the world. She had no patience for such things, especially when the sun was shining and the marsh was calling.

"I enjoy it," said her mom, "as much as you enjoy birding."

She caught the resentment in her mother's voice and felt a momentary twinge of guilt. Her mother took it as a personal insult when Tess complained about sewing. It wasn't Tess's thing. Why should Tess feel guilty?

But she did, and she resented it.

After a late breakfast, Tess grabbed her notebook and went down to Grandpa's study. It was her favourite room, perhaps because it was filled with her grandfather's belongings.

She liked to sit in his favourite leather chair and gaze at the painting above the fireplace. It was of a pair of sandhills dancing in the marsh at sunrise. The painting was huge — the length of the mantle above the fireplace — and whenever Tess looked at it, she thought of her grandfather's promise.

Someday, you'll see the cranes dance.

But how long could a promise last? Was it like love? Mom said love lasted for always. She said she loved Tess's dad, Bert, as much now as she had before he died. And that was ten years ago.

Then suddenly Tess remembered why she'd come downstairs. She hesitated for a moment before opening the drawer. Inside, she found a pile of old photographs, several field notebooks, a compass, and a heavy object wrapped in soft yellow flannel. She unwrapped the flannel and there it was: Grandpa's pocket watch! She held up the watch by its long silver chain. It was really beautiful, much nicer than her new plastic wrist watch. She pressed the pocket watch against her cheek. The silver felt cold and hard. She remembered how the watch chain had always hung from her grandfather's pocket. She felt a lump forming in her throat. Then she sighed and returned the watch to the drawer for safekeeping.

Glancing at the bird section of her grandfather's library, she chose three books about cranes. As she read, she discovered there were other people like her grandfather and Clara who spent their lives studying cranes and trying to protect them. She read about a wonderful river in Nebraska called the Platte. It was also called the crane river because thousands of sandhills nested along its banks.

But the crane population was shrinking because the Platte was drying up. The farmers were using too much water to irrigate their corn fields. The cranes' roosting areas were disappearing as the water levels dropped. The scientists were worried about the Platte, but the situation in the polder was worse.

Tess stared out the window, watching some Canada geese flying back and forth to a small swimming hole in the field. Grandpa called it Goose Pond because it was a favourite resting spot for geese in the area.

She heard footsteps down the hall. Then the door flew open.

"Hello, my dear," said Randall, stamping his feet. "It's freezing in this room. But that can be remedied in two shakes of a lamb's tail! I'm going to build a nice fire for you!"

"I'm fine. Really," said Tess.

"I insist."

Tess remembered the fires her grandfather used to build down by the slough. It was usually in late August when the nights got chilly. They'd sit on a log and watch the stars. She loved the crackle of the flames and the sizzle of the water spitting from the logs and the sweet cedar smell. And she'd always feel a little sad because summer was almost over.

Randall carried in an instant chemical log. He began whistling as he lit it at both ends of the wrapper.

Why couldn't he just leave her alone? He always seemed to find an excuse to interrupt her whenever she sat in Grandpa's study.

Outside, she heard loud honking. The call sounded different than the usual cackling of the Canada geese. It reminded her of the beep of an old-fashioned taxi. She picked up her binoculars and scanned the pond. A trumpeter swan! It had just landed near the edge of the water. A trumpeter was a good sighting! It was the first time she'd seen one, except in her grandfather's field guide. By summer, most of them had already flown north.

She opened her bird notebook and began to write.

May 11, 1:30 p.m. Willowcreek Farm

I just saw my first trumpeter! It looked like the swans I've seen in story books. It's pure white and very beautiful. Its bill was black. The trumpeter kept beeping at the flock of Canada geese. Now I know how it got its name! The swan kept dipping its neck and head down into the water. Most of the time, I could see only its white tail sticking up. It stayed under the water for a long time. It must have been eating water plants.

The geese were flapping their wings and cackling.

This is our pond, they seemed to say. Get out of here! But the trumpeter just ignored them. Then I saw someone walking along the dyke. The trumpeter looked startled and took flight. I noticed that it flew with its neck straight out like a crane.

21 Canada geese
2 buffleheads
1 trumpeter swan
Tess out.

Tess out. It sounded professional. For a moment she felt like a real birder, like Clara and Grandpa.

Uncle Randall stood beside her at the window.

"What a racket those birds make," he complained.

"How come you don't like birding, Uncle Randall?" asked Tess.

He shrugged. "Never had the inclination. I'm a doer, not a watcher."

It struck Tess as strange that neither her mother nor her uncle had any interest in something that had been so important to their father. She'd asked her mom about it on more than one occasion, but her mother would quickly change the subject.

When the instant log suddenly caught flame, Uncle Randall smiled.

"There, my dear. How's that?"

"It's uh ... nice. Thanks," said Tess.

She felt a little guilty now. He'd interrupted her, but he *had* made a fire for her. Even an instant fire was nice.

"Tessera," he said, clearing his throat.

"Yes?"

"I heard you coming up the stairs this morning."

"Oh." She might have known. He was going to lecture her.

"I don't know where you were and I'm not going to ask — this time. I do not wish to cause your mother more anxiety than she has already suffered. But as your uncle, I am responsible for your safety and I cannot, in all conscience, allow you to conduct yourself in such an irresponsible manner. Unexpected things can happen out there in the mists ... tragic things. If I catch you sneaking out again, I will report you immediately to your mother. It's for your own good."

You don't know what's good for me!

Randall tapped his fingers impatiently on the desk. He was waiting for her reply. But speaking her mind would only get her into more trouble.

"Okay," she said.

Her uncle sighed loudly, then turned on his heels.

· 9 ·

Tabi

CLARA'S INVITATION to visit was for Tuesday after school. Tess and Sally asked the school bus driver to drop them off at Clara's mailbox on Pitt Road. Though it was late afternoon, the May weather had already begun to warm. The air of the polder smelled green and sweet. As they walked down the long winding dirt road leading to the cabin, Tess could see the pink blossoms on the wild cranberry vines beginning to appear. The flowers looked like tiny shooting stars among the beds of sphagnum moss covering the bog.

Tess was curious about the bird woman. She sensed something mysterious, almost secretive, about her.

"Does Clara live by herself?" asked Tess.

"Yup," said Sally, matching Tess's step.

"She never got married?"

"Nope."

"I wonder if she ever gets lonely?"

"I would," said Sally. "There's always so many people at our house. It would seem too quiet."

"Maybe she likes being by herself," said Tess. Sometimes Tess felt more lonely when there was lots of people around than when she was alone. She wondered if Clara might feel that way, too.

"When's Zak coming?" asked Sally.

"As soon as he's finished his chores," said Tess.

On either side of the road were slough-filled ditches. The Labrador tea and hardhack bushes lining the road were alive with birds: marsh wrens, yellowthroats, red-winged blackbirds. The birds flitted from bush to bush, swinging on slender branches, feeding their babies, and shushing visitors if they came too close to their nests.

Clara's log cabin was surrounded by a sunny meadow. A buttercup meadow. The kind of meadow Uncle Randall hated. He called the flowers "noxious weeds," but Tess thought that nothing was prettier.

To the north of the cabin lay the Golden Ears Mountains and the Alouette River.

Approaching the meadow, they heard a loud puttering.

"Sounds like a crane!" said Tess.

The crane emerged from the dense underbrush a few feet away. It was so close Tess could almost touch it.

Suddenly, the crane retracted its long slender neck, lowered its head and spread out an enormous canopy of grey feathers.

"It's bowing," whispered Sally.

The crane flapped its wings, leaped, then performed another deep bow. On its way up, the bird tossed a small twig into the air and jabbed it with its beak. It bowed again and tossed up a piece of moss. Bow, toss and jab!

The crane began to leap into the air, gaining momentum with each successive bound. The crane's legs seemed made of rubber springs, bouncing so high Tess imagined the bird soaring into space.

Tess started to laugh. It was the most wonderful thing she'd ever seen.

Suddenly they heard a door slam. It was Clara.

The crane gave a loud whoop.

"Tabi, Tabi, Tabi!" cried Clara. "You're showing off again!"

The crane bounded towards the bird woman. From the crane's throat, Tess heard a low thrumming sound.

"What's that?" asked Sally.

"He's purring!" said Clara.

"I thought only cats purr," said Sally.

"Cranes too, if they're happy. It's called the contact call. Parents give it to their chicks or one of a crane pair will give it to the other."

Clara showed them how to make the soft rolling purr with their tongues.

"Try it," she said.

Tess purred. And to her surprise the crane answered her.

"He likes you," said Clara.

"Is he a pet?" asked Tess.

"More like a family member," replied Clara. "He wandered into my yard one day. I found him with the bantam chicks. His brother or sister must have driven him from the nest. He was dehydrated and half starved. He almost didn't make it. Poor little thing."

"How old is he?" asked Tess.

"Fourteen."

"That sounds old for a bird," asked Sally.

"It is," said Clara. "But cranes live longer than most birds. They can live up to twenty or thirty years in the wild. In captivity, they can live as long as humans."

Suddenly, Clara looked sad. "I dreamed that one day Tabi would join others of his kind. Every November, I'd release him at different places in the polder, Pitt Lake and the West Bog, places where I'd tracked the wild cranes. But the bird seemed bewildered by them. Several days later, Tabi would find his way back. There he'd be, scratching at my door. And I'd think, well, maybe next year. A few years ago, I gave up trying."

"Grandpa told me about that," said Tess. "He said that if a chick sees a person rather than its bird mother when it hatches, the bird will think the person is its mother."

"Exactly. It's called imprinting. When I began feeding Tabi, I became his mother. Now the rascal thinks he's human."

"What do you call him?" asked Sally.

"*Grus canadensis tabida*," said Clara. "The scientific name for the greater sandhill crane. Tabi for short."

"He's beautiful," sighed Tess.

They sat on a log watching Tabi catch flies. The flies were buzzing round a patch of skunk cabbage. The crane followed an insect, then scooped it up into his bill.

Finally, Zak arrived.

"Hi, everyone," he said, opening the front gate. "So that must be Tabi!"

"You knew about Tabi?" asked Tess.

Zak grinned. "My mom told me."

Sally and Tess exchanged looks.

"I didn't want to spoil Clara's surprise," said Zak.

He gave Tess a mischievous smile. He looked so cute when he smiled like that. Sometimes, she caught him staring at her in a certain way. If she didn't know better — it was obvious he was Rowena's boyfriend — she might have thought he liked her.

But he was just a friend and having a friend felt good.

Tabi put on quite a show. He approached Clara, standing erect, flapping his wings and making the contact call. Then he extended his wings and pointed his beak in the opposite direction.

"Not now!" said Clara, gruffly.

"What does he want?" laughed Zak.

"He wants me to dance," said Clara. "When he was a tiny downy, I was his dancing partner. We do a round or two every day, don't we, Tabi?"

"Aw. Dance with him," said Tess.

"Please!" said Sally.

Clara sighed.

"Shall we dance, Tabi?"

Clara began to flap her arms up and down and bow and leap in front of the skinny-legged bird. The crane trumpeted loudly, flapping his wings and bowing. The bird woman and the crane danced while Tess and Zak giggled.

Clara's face was growing redder by the minute and her breathing faster and louder, until suddenly the spry old woman threw herself onto the grass.

"Enough!" yelled Clara.

But Tabi didn't want to quit. He flapped his wings and and stamped his feet and uttered soft snuffling pleas.

"No, Tabi," said Clara, sitting up.

Tabi stared at Clara as if trying to comprehend. Then he suddenly flapped his wings and rose smoothly into the air, circled twice and landed with a loud whoop.

Clara groaned. "*Now* he wants me to fly. He's showing off because he has an audience."

"You can fly?" joked Zak.

Clara laughed. "I try, though I've never quite mastered the skill. But Tabi doesn't give up hope. I played the flying game with Tabi when he was a downy. I think he believes, if he's patient enough, I'll learn."

"Show us," pleaded Tess. "Just once."

"Just once, then."

Clara stood up, brushed herself off, and called to the crane.

"Okay, Tabi! Let's fly!"

Clara looked like a clown, flapping her arms up and down in the air and galloping alongside the skinny-legged, long-necked bird.

The crane made several leaps beside her, sprang into the air, circled, then landed with a loud whoop of pleasure, ready for the next round.

"That's the trouble," grumbled Clara. "That crane doesn't know when to quit. You kids have a go. Give me a rest."

"Not me," said Zak, looking embarrassed.

"No, no, no," said Sally.

"No thanks," said Tess shaking her head.

"How could you refuse him?" asked Clara mischievously. "Look at the poor creature."

Tabi squawked and puttered pathetically.

Tess looked at Tabi. The crane cocked his head to one side and stared at her. Her reserve melted.

"I'll try," said Tess, gingerly holding out her arms. She tried not to think about how silly she must look.

Tess's first flight was tentative, but Tabi's whoops of glee were soon contagious. Tess found herself enjoying the game, despite the laughter of her audience.

"Your turn," said Tess, issuing a challenge to Zak.

"Go on," said Clara. "That bird won't stop fussing until he's had his fill of it."

Zak accepted Tess's challenge reluctantly, at first. But

after several tries he threw himself into the game with enthusiasm. He imitated Tabi's high-pitched whoop perfectly.

"You make a great crane!" cried Tess.

Later, Sally *flew* with Tabi. Then finally, they all took flight. Tabi loved it.

"I've never in all my days seen such a rag-tag flock!" said Clara, shaking her head.

They couldn't stop laughing. The crane was like a retriever fetching a ball or a stick. He never seemed to tire of it. An hour later, the crane was just as eager, but the three of them were exhausted.

Then Clara showed them her property. Tabi came along, too, following a few feet behind. They saw her garden behind the house — one side for vegetables, recently planted, the other side for flowers — the tumbled down hen house beyond the garden, the willow by the tiny creek that wound through the meadow, and, beyond that, the marsh.

She showed them the incubators and explained to them how they worked.

They saw the hens and rooster and the rabbits, and they met Grump, Clara's pet skunk. The animal snarled at them as they passed.

"Don't worry. His stink sack has been removed," explained Clara.

There were birdhouses and hummingbird feeders hanging everywhere: from the eaves of the cabin, from the trees, from fence posts.

After the tour, Clara invited them into her kitchen.

"Outside, Tabi," she said, closing the door behind her. She turned to Tess. "He gets overly excited when I have guests."

As Clara served hot chocolate and homemade blueberry muffins, Tabi scratched at the door and bugled. Finally, Clara sighed and opened the door.

"Only if you behave yourself," said Clara wagging her finger at the bird. Tabi leapt inside, looking up at the ceiling, as if to say, *Me? You mustn't mean me?*

"He's been known to peck at things," said Clara under her breath. "Watch your shoes."

Tabi stationed himself beside Tess and chirped for crumbs. Tess hesitated, knowing how sharp a crane's bill is.

"He won't bite," said Clara.

Tess broke off a piece of her muffin and placed it on her hand. The crane scooped up the cake gently while Tess stared at the bird in fascination.

Tabi purred softly.

"You've found an admirer," said Clara.

"It's mutual," said Tess.

· 10 ·

Stormy Weather

THE FOLLOWING AFTERNOON a storm hit the polder. The rain fell in torrents, pounding loudly on the windows and rattling the shutters. As night fell, the temperature dropped and the rain turned to hailstones. Gusts of wind sent leaves, branches and roof tiles skittering across the ground.

By dawn, the storm was over, leaving the front lawn littered with broken branches.

That morning, Tess tossed her city shoes into the back of her closet. She pulled out a pair of fleece-lined black leather boots, a wool turtleneck sweater, jeans, and a raincoat.

By the time Tess arrived at the bus stop, the sun had broken through the clouds. Sally and Zak waved when they saw her. Rowena looked the other way.

"Clara broke her ankle," Zak told the girls when Tess approached.

"How did it happen?" asked Tess.

"She was outside during the storm. She fell over some windfall branches."

"Poor Clara," said Sally.

"Yeah," said Zak. "My mom told me this morning. Our next door neighbour, Bob Peters, drove her to the hospital."

"Is she still in the hospital?" asked Tess. Rowena pretended to ignore them, but she was obviously eavesdropping.

"Yes. She'll be home tomorrow, but her leg's in a cast."

"Who's going to take care of her?" asked Tess.

"I don't know," said Zak. "She has no family here. The Peters were worried. They wanted to help, but she turned them down."

Tess thought for awhile.

"I'm going to visit her when she gets home tomorrow," she said. "She's going to need help."

"Do you want me to go with you?" asked Zak.

"Sure. If you want to," said Tess.

She glanced at Sally.

"I can't," said Sally. "I promised my grandfather I'd go fishing with him. I'll go the next day, though."

Rowena edged closer.

"So ... what's happening tomorrow?" asked Rowena.

"We're visiting Clara Williams," said Zak.

"The bird woman? She's crazy!" said Rowena.

"You don't even know her," snapped Tess. "She broke her ankle and needs help."

Rowena glared at Tess. "It's sickening the way you follow Zak like a puppy dog."

"I ... I don't ..." stammered Tess.

"Yes, you do!" said Rowena. "Ever since you came here, you've done exactly that."

"Come on, Row," said Zak. "You can come, too, if you want."

"I wouldn't go if you begged me," said Rowena, folding her arms. She looked as though she were going to cry.

"I wish you'd both stop it," said Zak, walking away from them. He looked angry.

Gail put her arm around Rowena protectively.

Was Rowena right? wondered Tess. Was she chasing Zak?

"Rowena," called Sally, stepping forward. Sally's mouth was set in a stubborn line.

Rowena raised her eyebrows. "What?"

"Your problem," said Sally, "is that you have to be the centre of attention all the time and if anyone else gets any — like Tess — you're upset."

Rowena looked dumbstruck. Then she hissed, "Who pays attention to *her?*"

"Zak does," said Sally. "*That's* what bothers you."

Sally took Tess's arm. "Ignore her," she said.

The two girls walked up the road a little way, checking behind themselves every so often to see when the bus was coming.

"I can't stand that girl!" said Sally, as soon as they were out of earshot. "From the time I was in kindergarten, she's called me names. Brown skin, squaw-face, some others I won't repeat. Two years ago I got sick of her bullying — and I stood up to her. Told her what I thought of her." Sally laughed wryly. "She didn't change, but *I* feel a lot better now."

Tess fought back tears. "Sometimes when someone doesn't like me, I wonder if I've done something to deserve it. I think maybe there's something wrong with me. And if I'm quiet enough they won't notice. But it usually doesn't work."

"There's nothing wrong with you," said Sally, touching her shoulder.

"You don't know me," said Tess. "Sometimes I get so mad inside, I want to scream. I'm not as nice inside as I seem ... you know ... on the outside."

Sally laughed. "I figured that! But you're not like Rowena."

"I hope not."

"Friendship with someone like that is worthless," said Sally. "I used to go home crying because someone at school would call me names. I felt like I was no good. And my grandmother would say, 'Your spirit is suffering because you've put it in a cage. You've kept it too quiet. You've told it to be too good.' She said sometimes you need to howl like a coyote and look your enemy in the eye, like this." Sally bugged out her eyes and lolled her tongue.

Tess doubled over with laughter.

They heard a loud honk.

"There's the bus! I can see it at the corner. We'd better hurry."

Then, without saying another word, they began to howl. They howled like coyotes on a moonlit night, though it was still morning on the polder. It felt good.

· II ·

Discussions

"WALK IN! The door's unlocked," Clara called out. "Come through the kitchen. Go down the hallway. First door on your right."

Tabi was lying on a rug in front of the fireplace. The crane gave a loud whoop when he spotted them.

"Hello, Tabi!" said Tess. The bird rose to his feet, extending his wings, and began to purr.

"Listen, Zak. He's purring. I'm so glad to see you, Tabi. Yes I am. You're such a good boy."

Tabi followed them down the hallway, making strange tapping noises with his claws. The door opened into a sunny room filled with easels and paints and, except for a sofa and a chair facing the fireplace, little else. The log walls were covered with paintings. Some were of landscapes and flowers, but most were of birds: black-capped chickadees, marsh wrens, violet-green swallows, trumpeter swans, bald eagles, great blue herons, and sandhill cranes.

Clara was resting on the sofa. She had her leg propped up on a footstool. A pair of crutches lay beside her.

"Clara, I've been so worried about you!" cried Tess.

"Does it hurt?"

"Oh, it aches a little, but that's to be expected. I'm so happy to be home! I couldn't wait to get away from the hospital. Too many people hovering and fussing. I hate fusses! If I stayed there, I'd be feeling sorry for myself."

"Can we do anything for you?" asked Tess.

"You could autograph my cast!" she said.

Grump woke with a start, stretched, and, keeping his eyes fixed on Clara, raised his tail as if to spray them.

Clara gave the skunk a stern look and the animal went back to sleep.

"I didn't know you were an artist," said Zak, looking around. "Is this your studio?"

"In the winter," said Clara, "but I paint outdoors whenever I can."

"Do you have art shows?" asked Tess.

"Oh, yes. But I don't show my work around here. I have an agent who takes care of it."

"I love that one," said Tess, pointing to a large painting by the window.

The painting was of a single sandhill crane staring across a wide expanse of marsh. The bird seemed dwarfed by wetlands and sky.

"The crane looks real," said Zak.

Tess stared at the painting. There was something familiar about it. Maybe the crane's loneliness or maybe it was the subject matter — crane, marsh, sky.

Tess and Zak made a quick supper for Clara — some leftover soup and rolls — and Tess made a pot of tea.

Clara kept saying, "No need to fuss." But when she tried to walk on her crutches, Tess could see she was in pain.

Then Tess and Zak built a fire in the fireplace. And while the dampness in the room slowly disappeared, they talked about cranes.

Tabi sat beside Tess. He gave her a soft low purr, then tucked his head under his wing and went to sleep.

"By the time I get back on my feet," said Clara, "the downys will have hatched. I shouldn't have gone out in that storm. I love storms, can't resist them. They're grand dramas — like the sky performing opera!" She chortled at her joke, then grew serious. "But that was a bad one; I should have known better."

Suddenly Tabi lifted his head and stared at Tess. The bumpy red skin of his crown grew larger. Then, he sprang to his feet, flapped his wings and began to purr.

Tess purred in return.

"He wants to dance with you," said Clara.

Tess blushed.

"Clara's your dancing partner, Tabi," laughed Tess.

"That crane has no loyalty!" muttered Clara.

Tabi cocked his head to one side and let out an ear-splitting rattle.

"Hush, you rascal," said Clara, "or you'll be on the porch."

As if understanding, Tabi folded his legs under his body and tucked his head under his wing.

"Have you seen the newspaper?" asked Clara.

"No," said Zak.

"Is there news about the rezoning?" asked Tess.

"There's an editorial saying that the zoning bylaw should be approved," said Clara. "The development will save the community! There'll be money and jobs and everyone will be happy, happy, happy! No mention about the loss of wetlands! No mention about an endangered species. No mention about losing the best air quality control system ever invented!"

Clara was breathing hard. Her face was as red as Tabi's crest.

"What air quality control system?" asked Zak, looking puzzled.

"Why the marsh! It's like a giant sponge. It filters out air pollution. All our wonderful wetland plants, the spaghnum mosses, Labrador tea, sweet gale, and hardhack absorb lead and carbons from car exhaust and other pollutants. Then they change the toxic substances into non-toxic ones. It's the best sewage system in the world! But there's a catch."

"What's the catch?" asked Tess.

"The toxins will remain stored only if our marshes and bogs are undisturbed. If people dig them up, these pollutants will be released back into our air and water."

"I didn't know that," said Zak.

"Me neither," said Tess.

"Many people don't," said Clara. "And they don't know that wetlands prevent floods." Clara sighed. For a moment, Tess saw discouragement in Clara's eyes.

"How do they do that?" asked Zak.

"A wetland is like a huge storage tank for water," said Clara. "When it rains, wetland plants, like sphagnum moss, absorb up to twenty times their weight in moisture. Then during dry periods, these plants gradually release the water." Clara winked at Tess. "And this marvellous invention was invented by a woman!"

"Mother Nature!" volunteered Tess.

"Of course!"

"Do you think the developers will convince the council?" asked Tess.

"I don't know, Tess," said Clara, sadly. "Few people show up at the council meetings. It's not that they don't care. It's just that ... everyone's so busy. Developers work on these things quietly. It's only later, when people see what they've lost, that they want to do something. But, by then, it's too late."

"Uncle Randall says development is inevitable," said Tess.

Clara sighed. "Randall believes it, too. That's understandable after what happened to his family."

Tess was taken aback. "What do you mean?"

"Oh dear," said Clara. "I've spoken out of turn. This whole thing is too upsetting. I can't think straight. Don't ask me anything else. Just don't be too hard on your uncle. He hasn't had it easy. That's all."

Clara's tone was final. Yet, it was obvious the bird woman knew something about her family that she didn't want to share. Why was Clara reluctant to tell her? And why had neither her mother nor her grandfather told her? Tess felt a surge of resentment. Why did her family keep secrets from her? She was no longer a child.

· 12 ·

Secret Plans

IT'S ONLY LATER when people see what they've lost ... but by then it's too late.

Tess carried Clara's words with her for the next few days — as she rode on the bus and listened to her teacher and talked to her friends. Later at night, these thoughts weighed so heavily in her mind, she couldn't sleep. The development meeting was two months away. Time was running out for the cranes. They couldn't wait until Clara's ankle healed.

Then one night Tess had a wonderful dream. She dreamed she was holding a crane egg in her hand. And for the first time in days she felt happy.

That's when she made her decision. She had to help the cranes no matter how crazy it seemed. But she couldn't do it alone.

The next day at school, Tess asked Sally and Zak to eat lunch with her out by the back field.

"You should have seen Rowena's face when she saw you pass that note to Zak," said Sally.

"It's the only way I ever get to talk to him," said Tess.

"She clings to him like a limpet."

Sally laughed. "You mean, those sea creatures that stick on rocks?"

"Yeah."

"What's the secret? I won't tell."

"I'll tell you when Zak gets here."

"Hi, girls," said Zak, several minutes later. "Are we going ghost-hunting again?"

"No," said Tess. "Something more important."

"Oh?"

"But don't answer right away, okay?"

"Oh — kay," said Zak and Sally, exchanging looks.

"Promise?"

"Tell us. I can't stand the suspense," said Sally.

Tess took a deep breath. "We have to steal the crane eggs."

No response.

"Clara can't do it and there's no one else. The cranes need help."

Silence.

"I can't do it by myself," said Tess. She heard a soft whine in her own voice. Yuk! But she was prepared to beg if she had to.

"We don't have permission," said Zak.

"Clara does," said Tess, "and we'll take the eggs to her place as soon as we get them. I've brought some books on raising cranes. Here." She took three books from her backpack. "We could read up on how to do it."

For a moment, her own doubts came rushing back. Would her grandfather have taken a crane egg under these circumstances? She wasn't sure. But he would have done something.

"But a wild crane's not like Tabi," said Zak. "It could be dangerous."

"I thought you loved danger," said Tess.

"Within reason," said Zak.

"I know I'll be scared," said Tess. "But I'm willing to take the risk."

Tess turned to Sally. "Do you think it's a crazy idea?"

"Yup. But I'll do it."

"Oh, Sally! You're the greatest, most wonderful friend in the world."

She hugged Sally tightly.

Tess looked up at Zak. "It would be easy if there were three of us. One person could be the lookout. Someone else could distract the crane's attention. Then a third person could take the egg."

"Do I get to steal the egg?" asked Zak.

"Oh, all right," said Tess. She'd been hoping to capture the egg herself. But what really mattered was helping the cranes.

"Okay," said Zak. "I'll do it."

"Yippeee!" said Tess, leaping into the air. Then she hugged Sally again.

"Where's *my* hug?" teased Zak.

Tess didn't know what to say. She felt her cheeks burning.

Zak had his hands on his hips and that crooked smile on his face. And he was looking at her in a way that made her feel all shivery.

"Sally got a hug," he continued. "You're not prejudiced against guys, are you?"

Tess caught Sally's eye. She was smirking.

"All right," said Tess.

Zak walked over to her and put his arms around her. She'd never realized how tall he was before. She could hear her own heart pounding.

Tess gave Zak a shy smile, then pulled away.

"We could take the egg this weekend. On Saturday," said Tess.

"Okay," said Zak.

"I can go, if it's really early," said Sally. "I'm going fishing that day."

"You'll be back in lots of time," said Tess. "We'll have to meet before dawn. Meanwhile, let's find out more about raising baby cranes. Then we'll make our plans."

Tess handed Sally and Zak each a book.

Tess had already spent most of the night searching through her grandfather's books for answers. Many of the words seemed foreign to her. *Downy.* The word was as soft as down feathers. Other words she'd never heard before — *carunculated, pipped, mandibles* — the language of "crane."

They read while they ate.

Tess flipped through a book with torn, yellowing pages.

"Listen to this." She began reading aloud. "*The female usually lays two eggs ...* We could raise one chick and the crane parents could raise the other one. Hey, look at this!"

Tess could hardly contain her excitement. There in the book was a series of photographs showing how scientists used bantam hens to rear crane chicks until the baby cranes grew too tall for their caretakers.

"Clara's got bantams!" said Zak excitedly.

"I know!" said Tess.

"We could do that," said Sally.

Tess hesitated. "Wait a minute."

"What?" asked Zak.

"It says here that when the downys hatch, the first thing they have to see is marsh. They have to recognize the marsh as their home."

"But the marsh is behind Clara's house," said Zak. "Why would that be a problem?"

"Because the entrance to the henhouse is facing the cabin," said Tess. "The first thing the chick would see is the cabin. It would think the cabin was its home."

Zak thought for awhile.

"You know, if we got a wooden box, filled it with straw and nailed it to the wall of the henhouse facing the marsh, then we could put a crane egg in the box, place the bantam on the egg, and when the chick hatched, the first thing it would see is marsh."

"That might work," said Tess, "except for one thing."

"What's that?"

"The chick would have no protection from the weather or from predators."

"It would if the box had a hinged door," said Sally. "I could make a box with a door."

Zak looked surprised.

"It's not hard," said Sally. "I've been helping my grandfather build a shed and we have lots of extra wood."

"But the chicks won't be able to see the marsh with a door," said Zak.

"That's true," said Sally.

"Wait!" cried Tess. "I have an idea. Uncle Randall has a roll of strong transparent plastic at home. Maybe you could make a plastic door with a wooden frame. Then the chick could see the marsh, but it would also be protected."

"Leave it to me," said Sally with a smile.

"But ... if a coyote or raccoon were really persistent, they might be able to break into the box."

"I guess that could happen," said Tess. "Anything is possible, but it's worth a try."

Tess looked at Zak, then at Sally.

"Yes!" they said at the same time.

"Can you start the box tomorrow?" asked Zak.

"I'll start it today, after school," said Sally.

"Then we can take the egg three days from now," said Tess.

Looking up, she saw Rowena and Gail watching them from a distance.

· 13 ·

Operation Crane

FRIDAY EVENING, Tess packed her backpack with a rubber groundsheet and a half-eaten package of gingersnaps, then wrote a reminder to herself: DON'T FORGET BROOMS. She set her alarm for four a.m. — an hour before dawn — just enough time to settle in the blind, before the male crane joined his mate.

When Tess woke, it was raining, a cold wintry rain, unlike the drizzle of the spring. Black clouds curtained the moon, veiling the polder in thick grey shadows.

Walking to the dyke road behind Willowcreek Farm, she felt her doubts return.

What if the crane pair became frightened and abandoned the nest? She shivered at the thought. But it was harder to do nothing.

The marsh was silent, except for the mournful trill of the frogs and the swish of the wet grass against her jeans. Slowly, her doubts gave way to fear. She imagined coyotes, snakes, bloodsuckers.

Zak and Sally were standing on the dyke road. They waved at her.

"What are the brooms for?" asked Zak.

"To fool the cranes into thinking we're bigger," said Tess, handing him one. "They'll be less likely to attack."

Sally groaned at the word "attack."

"But I'm *sure* they won't," said Tess. "They'll probably try and lead us away from the nest."

As they walked towards the blind, their boots made loud sucking noises with each step, sinking deeper into the ground, which became softer as they got closer to the slough.

Rain plastered Zak's hair to his head and large drops of water clung to his eyelashes. Sally's rain slicker made a rustling sound as it rubbed against the soaked denim of her jeans.

Tess led the way, walking down the grassy slope of the dyke into a tangle of hardhack bushes below the dyke road. The branches were dense, providing a good cover for the cranes.

The blind was located about ten metres from the water's edge. Between the blind and the slough, the shore was a mass of soft mud covered with goose scat. It was a spot her grandfather had warned her about. The mud was unstable, almost like quicksand. But it was the only way to get to the island. If they were going to take the crane egg, they had no choice.

When Tess entered the blind, she took out a rubber groundsheet from her backpack and spread it over the grass.

"Come in," she said with mock politeness. Zak and

Sally crawled down beside her. Then Tess held up a larger groundsheet over her head and the three of them used it as a makeshift tent. It wasn't perfect, but it helped to keep off the rain.

Zak checked his watch. "We've got three-quarters of an hour before dawn," he said.

Sally shuddered. "I'll distract the first crane, Tess, if you'll be lookout."

"Why don't you let me go first?" asked Tess. She felt a sense of uneasiness in her stomach. What if something happened to Sally? She'd never forgive herself.

"I want to get it over with," said Sally. "The longer I wait, the more scared I get."

"Did you finish making the boxes?" asked Zak.

"They're at Clara's," said Sally.

"Did she see you?"

"Nope. I snuck round the back. They're all ready. I even put straw in them."

No one spoke for a long time.

"I wish it wasn't raining," sighed Zak.

Tess didn't reply. She folded her arms and tried to ignore the slow trickle of moisture seeping down her collar.

This time, she didn't mind the weather. She liked the thick darkness, the persistent tapping of the rain on the groundsheet. She liked leaning against Zak's shoulder and feeling the warmth of Sally's breath against her cheek. All three dozed off from time to time.

Once, Zak stirred from sleep and glanced at Tess through the grey light. He looked surprised for a moment, as if he'd forgotten where he was. She gave him a shy look, then closed her eyes.

Dawn arrived to a chorus of Wilson's warblers, their high musical *chip-chip-chip* rousing Tess from her sleep.

"Wake up," whispered Tess, tapping Zak and Sally on the shoulder.

Tess peered through the opening in the front of the blind. She could see the crane nest on the sandbar in the middle of the slough. From the blind, the nest looked to be about forty metres away. Its location was ideal; surrounded by water, the crane eggs would be safe from coyotes and foxes.

Then Tess saw something move. It was the hen crane sitting on the nest! The bird's feathers had blended in so well with the marsh grass that she had almost missed it.

Seconds later, a loud *garoo-a-a-a* sounded in the distance.

"Look!" said Tess. "I can see the male. He's flying in from the west bog."

They sat in silence, following the crane's flight across the sky, then his slow glide downward into a thicket.

"He's behind us," whispered Sally. "To the right."

The male called again, but this time Tess heard the female's higher pitched cry.

The guard call, thought Tess. Maybe she senses we're here.

"Better go now, Sally," said Zak.

"What if the hen won't leave the nest?" asked Sally.

"She will," said Tess. Her voice sounded more confident than she felt.

"Okay, I'm going." Sally looked pale. She slowly rose to her feet, holding the broom above her head.

"Walk carefully," warned Zak.

"And stand your ground," added Tess. "Remember, you can't outrun a crane."

Sally nodded. She walked slowly towards the shoreline of the slough, the broom swaying above her. She looked scared.

Suddenly the hen lowered her head and flattened her body on the nest. Curling her neck around her body, the crane lay her head on her wing.

"It looks like the hen's sleeping," said Zak. "I can hardly see her now."

"She senses danger. She's trying to hide."

"I wonder what she'll do when she sees Sally?"

"I hope she runs away."

When the hen spotted Sally, the bird rose above the eggs and with small furtive steps slunk through the bushes.

"Hey!" said Zak. "That was easier than I thought."

Sally waved. She had a smile on her face.

A few seconds later, the hen uttered a series of warning cries.

The guard call again, thought Tess. It's not over yet.

A strange hollow ratcheting sound emerged from the

bushes near the dyke road. This time Tess recognized the deeper voice of the male. Sally was sandwiched between two cranes, the female standing guard on the shore and the male hiding behind her in the hardhack bushes.

The crane pair repeated their high-pitched warnings which rang more and more urgently with each sequence.

Sally glanced back at Tess. Her face looked pale and her eyes large. She mouthed the word "help."

Don't panic, Sally, whatever you do. I can't help you. Two of us out there might cause the cranes to abandon the nest.

Tess tried to look calm. She motioned for Sally to continue.

Sally grimaced, then walked steadily towards the female.

Suddenly, the hen let out a high drawn-out putter, flew a short distance, then opened her wings and began to drag them across the vegetation.

Tess adjusted the spotting scope.

"She's using the injured wing trick."

"She's pretty convincing," said Zak. "A predator would think she was an easy target."

"And in the meantime, she's led her enemy away from her eggs."

"There goes Sally!"

Sally gave a thumbs up signal just before she followed the "wounded" crane into the bushes. Both girl and crane disapppeared from view.

Tess peered out. The male crane was standing behind the blind, his eyes fixed on the nest. Luckily, she and Zak remained hidden behind the narrow wall of branches on the open side of the blind.

"I should go now," said Tess, grabbing her broom.

"Be careful," Zak called after her.

Tess emerged from the blind, holding the broom above her head.

The male swung its neck in Tess's direction, then froze, staring at her. She remembered reading: *The male crane is more aggressive and territorial than the female.*

There were always exceptions, thought Tess hopefully. Maybe this was one.

The crane followed her with his eyes — large black pupils ringed with brilliant yellow. Tess kept walking, her back to the slough. The bird seemed to dare her to come closer. She took smaller and smaller steps, not wanting to give way.

I'm playing chicken with a crane, she thought. She hoped the bird wouldn't try to be a hero. She was now within kicking distance of the crane's powerful legs, legs strong enough to knock down a grown man. What would she do if the crane decided to defend his nest to the death?

Suddenly the crane spread his wings wide and ruffled his feathers in an attempt to frighten her.

Tess felt her chest begin to heave. Sensing her panic, the crane lunged towards her. He opened his beak wide, then slammed it into the mud, flapping his wings furiously. She froze.

The crane began to bound, circling Tess in tighter and tighter rings.

Loud gurgling rasps burst from the bird's trachea — unearthly sounds that sent waves of fear through Tess's body. Phrases from her grandfather's books on cranes flashed vividly in her mind: ... *a bill strong enough to crush bones of rodents or frogs, powerful enough to break a man's arm, sharp enough to tear snake hide.*

The crane moved closer. His neck twisted into a large S that wavered with each step. Tess saw the sharp edges of the crane's mandibles and the pecking motions of his bill. She shut her eyes and held her breath.

· 14 ·

Near Disaster

THE CRANE SQUAWKED loudly. Tess's eyes flew open. The bird gave her an indignant look, flapped its wings, then turned and disappeared into the hardhack. Sally was somewhere in the bushes. What if the male or the female caught Sally off guard?

Tess scanned the brush, but saw no movement. She signalled to Zak. Then she ran for cover behind some willow bushes about six metres from the water's edge.

Zak left the blind, checked both directions, and ran past her. She whispered "Good luck," but he didn't hear her. As he drew closer to the muddy shore, he slowed his steps.

Good, thought Tess, he's being cautious.

Holding her breath, she watched him step into the muck. With each tentative step, the mud rose round his boots, pulling him off balance. The mud was like quicksand. As soon as he got one foot unstuck, the other would become stuck.

When he reached the water's edge, Tess crossed her fingers. She hoped the slough bottom would be more stable.

Zak held out his arms to balance himself, testing the depth of the water before taking each step. The water rose past his knees, then past his waist.

Tess remembered her mother's warnings: *Stay away from the sloughs. They're dangerous.*

Each step Zak took placed him at risk. Tess hadn't realized how great a risk, until now. Just a few more steps, she said to herself. Just a few more. Then, finally, Zak was standing on the sandbar. He had a look of relief on his face. The ground seemed firm and he made his way to the nest quickly. The next moment, he held the egg in one hand.

Unable to contain herself, Tess crawled out from her hiding place. She smiled, then waved. Zak waved in response, but he didn't smile. Something was wrong.

Tess watched him go back into the water. That's when she noticed the colour of his lips. They were blue.

Hypothermia. It only takes minutes.

Her grandfather's words.

She felt so helpless, watching him from the shore. If anything happened to Zak, it would be her fault. The water rose around him. One moment it was up to his chest, the next his head had disappeared.

He came up choking and thrashing, one hand waving above him. He was trying to save the crane egg!

Tess grabbed the broom and rushed towards him. When she reached the shoreline, the muck sucked at her boots. She kept moving until she entered the water. She felt a sudden sting of cold as the icy water seeped into her boots and soaked her jeans. The pockets of her raincoat filled with water, weighing her down. Her limbs felt wooden, paralyzed by a cold that was sharper and more cutting than a knife. She wanted to cry out, but she gritted her teeth instead, adrenaline propelling her forward.

"Grab the broom," she yelled.

Zak lunged towards it, but his grasp was too short.

Tess took another step. The bottom shifted. She felt herself slipping.

"Don't come any closer," he warned. "It's like quicksand here."

"Let the egg go," she said. "Please."

The egg was important, but she couldn't let Zak drown.

"I can't," he rasped.

She leaped towards him, grabbing him by the jacket. He clutched at her, dragging her under. Freezing water entered her mouth. Her body felt numb. Retching from the taste of sludge and duckweed, she found herself standing on a partially level bottom.

"Take ... the egg," said Zak weakly. "I'm too ... tired."

Tess cupped her hand under Zak's and felt the smooth oval of the egg's contours. Then she pulled on Zak's jacket with every bit of strength she had left. She felt him steady himself.

"I'm okay," he said. "Take care of the egg."

"Are you sure?"

"Yes. Go ahead." He sounded angry. Tess didn't argue. She carried the egg as if the slightest movement would cause it to break into a million pieces.

As Tess took her first few steps on firm ground, Sally came running up. They turned to check on Zak who was lying in the muck, exhausted. He was covered in black silt and dead vegetation.

A hoarse wheezing sound came from the thicket. The male crane was running towards them.

"Watch out," yelled Zak, scrambling to his feet.

They bolted past the crane to the blind, where all three collapsed.

"What happened?" Sally asked.

"It's like quicksand out there," gasped Tess. "We both fell in."

"But we got the egg!" panted Zak. Suddenly, he grinned. "I've got some good news, too."

"What?" asked Tess.

"There were three eggs in the nest."

"That's terrific!" said Sally. "That makes one more crane chick than we expected."

"Clara will be pleased," said Tess.

"Let me hold the egg," said Sally. She turned the egg round in her hand. "It's bigger than I thought. Way bigger than a hen's egg. Prettier, too."

Tess glanced at Zak. His body was shaking with the cold.

"We've got to get you home," said Tess. "You've been in the water too long."

"Yeah, you look bad," added Sally. Handing Tess the egg, she took off her jacket. "Put this on."

"I'm fine," said Zak.

"No, you're not," said Sally. "You're shaking like a leaf. That's glacier water. One of my cousins died from a boating accident. He didn't drown. He died of the cold."

Tess saw a flicker of alarm in Zak's eyes. He put Sally's jacket on.

Tess took a cloth from her backpack and wrapped the egg. Then they headed home as fast as they could.

Zak looked at Sally. "Too bad you didn't join us for a swim," he joked.

Sally laughed. "Yes, I arrived a little too late. But I was busy keeping that crane out of mischief. Did you see how I stared it down? Showdown between girl and crane! Girl wins!"

"Gr-r-r-reat job, Sally," said Zak.

When they reached the fork in the dyke road, Tess and Zak said goodbye to Sally. Then they walked to Tess's place. Zak lived a quarter mile farther down the road.

"You'd better get home," said Tess.

"Are you trying to get rid of me?" asked Zak. There was that crooked smile again. She felt like melting every time she saw it.

"No, I'm just worried you'll get pneumonia."

"I'm going," he said, shivering. "Thanks for what you did. I was in trouble out there."

"I know."

"You've got duckweed in your hair," said Zak and, reaching over, he pulled several long green strands out. "I can hardly move my fingers, they're so cold."

"Get going," said Tess.

"You're taking the egg to Clara's?" he asked.

"As soon as I get changed."

"I'll talk to you later," he said. Then he turned and ran down the driveway.

· 15 ·

On the Home Front

TESS HEARD A COUGH. Her uncle was standing behind the front door as she entered.

"What have you been up to, young lady?" he boomed.

"Ah ... I was ... down by the slough."

"That's rather obvious," he said. "What's that?"

"What?"

"Whatever it is you're trying to hide. Right there."

"Oh, that."

"What is it?"

"Just an egg."

"An egg?"

"A crane egg," said Tess, finally.

Randall shook his head. "You're just like my father. Always trying to save something, aren't you. Eagles, herons, cranes. He loved birds more than people," he said bitterly.

Tess felt her blood boil.

That's not true! My grandfather loved people.

"What happened?" asked her mother as she came to the doorway. Her voice seemed on the verge of hysterics. "Look at you!"

Tess drew back. She'd never seen her mother so upset. "You were down by the slough, weren't you? Weren't you!"

"Yes," sighed Tess. She hated how her mother constantly worried. But this time Tess had no defence. She'd put herself at risk and her friends, too.

"What happened?" asked Marjory, her voice finally calm.

"I fell into the slough."

Tess stared at her feet. Her wet clothes had formed a puddle around her.

"How many times have I warned you? A million at least! What were you doing near the slough?"

"Marjory, I am obliged as Tessera's uncle to inform you that your daughter has been sneaking out on the polder with a young man ... while we have been sleeping. And I see your daughter's outings have been occurring without your permission."

Marjory's mouth fell open.

"Tess! Is this true?"

"Zak McIver and I are friends," said Tess. "And Sally was there, too."

"But what were you *doing* out there?" asked her mother.

"I ... we wanted to ... Clara broke her ankle and she couldn't do it ..." Her words were coming out wrong. What was the use. Her mother wouldn't understand.

Randall shook his head impatiently. "Bird egg. That's what she's trying to say. She's holding it."

Tears sprang into her mother's eyes. Her face grew pale. "You could have died from the cold. Or drowned." She slumped into the nearest chair.

"We were really careful. And the crane egg was worth it. We're going to raise a baby crane!"

Marjory shook her head in disbelief. "What will you think of next?"

"Did your friends secure permission from their parents?" Randall asked.

"Not ... exactly," said Tess.

"Then your mother must inform their parents," said her uncle. "It is her responsibility."

"Please, Mom, don't," begged Tess.

"Randall's right."

"But ..."

"End .... of .... discussion," said her mother. "You're shivering. Now get those wet clothes off and have a hot bath."

Just for once she'd like to see her mother take her part. But she never did.

Marjory phoned Zak's and Sally's parents and she got even more upset when she found out the details. Zak had made their adventure sound more exciting by telling his mother they'd nearly drowned in the quicksand. He hadn't realized it would make things worse for Tess.

But Sally's mother managed to calm Marjory down. She convinced Tess's mother that experiences in nature were important for girls and that these experiences built confidence and independence. It was the mention of independence that finally won over Tess's mother. But she still thought Tess should be grounded.

"Anything but grounding," protested Tess. "I'll do chores instead. I'll do an hour every day for a whole week. I'll do vacuuming, dusting, laundry — anything you like. I have to get the egg to Clara's as soon as possible or it might not hatch. And Clara needs help, too. She's still got her cast on."

"You should be grounded," said her mother.

"But the egg ... and Clara ..."

"Okay," said Marjory grudgingly.

"Thanks!" said Tess. "I'll do my chores as soon as I get back. Promise."

As Tess walked to Clara's, she thought about her mom. She had never been able to figure her out. In some ways, her mother was extremely independent. When Tess's father died, she started a dressmaking business and managed to support herself and Tess without anyone's help. She made a point of telling Tess that. And Tess remembered her grandfather offering to send them money on many occasions, but her mom had always refused. She had always said a woman should make her own way.

But in other ways, Marjory was anything but independent. She seemed fearful, afraid of anything beyond the back garden. What else would explain her continual warnings?

"Don't go too far from the house." "Stay away from the sloughs." When Tess got home after birding, her mother always had a look of relief on her face.

"Why do you worry so much?" Tess would ask irritably.

And her mom would reply, "Because I care about you."

But Tess hated her mother's overprotectiveness. She felt suffocated, as though she were locked in a sealed room on a sunny day. It was strange how Tess felt imprisoned indoors, where her mother felt safe. That's how they were different.

A Difficult Dance

As Tess approached Clara's cabin, she heard guitar music, singing and clapping. Tess was surprised. She'd expected Clara to be resting.

No one answered her knock, so she followed the music to Clara's studio. The music sounded like the gypsy music her grandfather had often played. It made her feel happy and sad all at once.

Opening the door, she spied Clara's long white hair and her leg cast swaying. One crutch was tucked neatly under her arm, while the other one swept the air to the beat.

"Po rum pum pum, pe rum pum pe rum pum pero perum," sang Clara. Her voice sounded slightly off-key. But the song sounded lively and dramatic.

Suddenly, Tess heard a loud puttering. It was Tabi leaping to the music.

When Tabi spotted her, he began to twirl with excitement, pecking at the air. He flapped his wings so rapidly a pile of books fell onto the floor.

Clara looked up, startled.

"Well, look who's here! Turn off the music and we'll

have a visit."

"You don't have to stop," said Tess.

"I'm all worn out now. Dancing's a trifle difficult with crutches," said Clara. "But Tabi doesn't settle until he does a few rounds."

Clara eased herself carefully into a chair, sliding her crutches onto the floor.

"You two looked so funny," said Tess.

Clara grinned. "Did you hear that, Tabi? I'd accept 'graceful' or 'inspiring' — but 'funny'?"

"I didn't mean it, Tabi," said Tess. "You're the finest dancer in the polder, maybe even in the universe!"

Tabi began to purr.

"What have you got there?" asked Clara.

"Something special," said Tess, placing the small bundle on Clara's lap.

Clara unwrapped the egg carefully.

It was twice the size of a hen's egg in a soft beige with lavender, pale green, and brown markings.

Clara's eyes grew wide.

"Crane egg! Where did you get it?"

"From the nest behind my place."

Clara's hand went to her throat.

"By yourself?"

"Sally and I distracted the cranes, while Zak took the egg."

"Did the cranes return to the nest?" asked Clara. The

frown line between her eyes suddenly became a deep furrow.

Tess felt her cheeks grow warm.

"I'm ... not sure. We left right away."

Clara's hands fluttered around her. "Oh, dear. Oh, dear. I hope the cranes don't abandon the nest."

Did I do the wrong thing?

Suddenly, Tess felt like crying. If she had frightened the cranes off she'd never forgive herself. She stared at her feet, searching for the right words to explain to Clara. She wanted the bird woman to understand.

"I wanted to help. I thought if the scientists could do it ..."

How could she think such a thing? She was in grade seven. What could she do?

"There. There," said Clara, patting her hand. "Your heart was in the right place. No denying that. But you put yourself in danger. Your friends, too. And if the cranes abandon the nest ..."

"... then their eggs will never hatch," said Tess. "I will have harmed the cranes, not helped them."

Tess picked at a hangnail on her thumb. She felt a sharp pain as she tore off the tiny piece of skin. She wanted to disappear. She hadn't thought of the negative consequences.

"I know what you're thinking, Tess. If it's okay for Clara to take a crane egg from the nest and raise it, why not you?"

That's what she'd thought then. But not now.

Clara's face softened. "I don't know a birder alive today

who wouldn't have doubts about stealing a mama bird's egg," continued Clara. "But you have to know what you're doing. And even then, a million things could go wrong! It's such a big responsibility for three kids."

"We're already carrying it," said Tess, staring down at the egg.

The bird woman reached for the egg and touched it gently.

"Warm to the touch. A good sign."

Tess's eyes met the old woman's. Her eyes were small and dark. Barn owl eyes set into a soft, white, heart-shaped face.

"Maybe I've underestimated you," said Clara. She reached over and squeezed Tess's hand. "Maybe you *do* realize how important this is."

"I do," said Tess. And for once her voice sounded strong and firm.

"Hold the egg up to the light," said Clara.

Tess saw a flicker of a smile at the corner of the bird woman's lips.

"Crane eggs are so beautiful, aren't they?" sighed Clara.

"Yes," said Tess. "Guess how many eggs were in the crane's nest?"

"Two?"

"No."

"Three?" asked Clara hopefully.

"Yes!"

"What a stroke of luck!" said Clara.

Then she waved her hands in the air. "No time for day-dreaming. Put the egg over by the wood stove for now. On the shelf. Not too close. Incubator. That's what we'll need. Now where did I put it? Think now, Clara."

"We won't need the incubator, if one of your bantams sits on the egg," said Tess. "Sally built a wooden box with a hinged door. We filled it with straw and turned it so the box is facing the marsh."

"Well, well, well," said Clara. "You three have thought of everything."

"Wouldn't it be wonderful to watch the baby crane fly south in the fall?"

Clara looked surprised.

"Tess, you can't get your hopes up like that. The chances are slim that the crane will be wild. It *could* happen, and that's what we're hoping for. But more often than not, it doesn't. Even if the bantam hatches the egg, we'll have to help the hen feed and care for the chick. And that means the baby will imprint on us."

"You mean it will be tame?"

"Perhaps not as tame as Tabi," said Clara gently. "But it may not fit in with its own kind. The chances of it migrating or of having a family are slim."

Then she saw Tess's face. "But a chance is better than nothing."

"I hope it lives and has a family," said Tess.

"I had hopes for Tabi, but it never happened. I became his family. Sometimes I wonder if I should have rescued him."

"Don't say that, Clara!"

"Oh, I'm just feeling down today. I was hoping Tabi's dancing would cheer me up. But not today."

"What's wrong?" asked Tess.

"Read the article on the front page," said Clara, handing Tess the newspaper.

MARSHWORLD BRASS VISITS PITT MEADOWS

Marshworld plans to utilize the beauty of the polder. The entertainment park's theme would be the marsh and all its creatures. Randall De Boer, a spokesperson for a group of developers, cautioned that the zoning has to be changed before anything concrete happens. According to De Boer, "We're at the talking stage right now but the theme park officials are impressed by the area."

"Your uncle's making quite a splash, isn't he?" said Clara.

Tess didn't answer. She could almost taste her anger. It was like sandpaper against the inside of her mouth. She wondered if it was wrong to feel that way.

Her eyes fell upon the painting of the sandhills. There was something about it that always startled her.

"The painting in Grandpa's study!"

Clara flushed.

"*You* did it!" said Tess.

Clara's words were measured.

"I gave your grandfather a painting when I was in my twenties," she said. "I'm surprised he kept it all these years."

"Were the two of you good friends?" asked Tess excitedly.

"Oh goodness, that was so long ago," and Clara dismissed the subject with a wave of her hand.

Tess was curious. Why would Clara give Grandpa a painting? And why had she failed to mention it? Sometime soon, she'd have to discuss it further with Clara. But right now Tess had other things on her mind.

She blew farewell kisses to Tabi.

"So long, Clara," she said.

Then she took the crane egg to the bantam. The bantam craned her neck to get a peek at the strange-looking egg beneath her, shifted her weight and immediately accepted her responsibility.

Tess was relieved. Yet when she left Clara's cabin, she couldn't shake the feeling that there was more trouble ahead.

· 17 ·

A New Approach

"I CAN'T BELIEVE you've let her off grounding," growled Randall. "You're too soft on her."

"She misses her Grandpa," said Marjory. "He was like a father to her."

"He was more of a father to *her* than he was to *us*," said her uncle.

Tess was sitting on the stairs listening. She hated when her uncle talked about Grandpa like that. She wondered if he were lying.

"Maybe ... he saw Tess needed him," said Tess's mom.

"I needed him, too," said her uncle, his voice cracking.

Tess sighed. She couldn't listen any more. Dragging herself downstairs, she went to the laundry room and began her chores. Today she had to fold laundry, vacuum, and dust as she had promised.

She found the book when she was vacuuming her grandfather's study. It was wedged between the back of the leather chair and the bookcase. It was called *The Cranes and Their Allies* and was written by Wallace Rallings, the famous birder and scientist, a man her grandfather had often mentioned. The spine of the book still felt stiff and the pages unworn. It looked new.

She turned the vacuum off and sat down with it. Grandpa must have been reading it shortly before he died.

She flipped through the pages until she came to a photo of a scientist in a crane suit. He had a puppet on his hand. The puppet looked just like a sandhill crane. It was made from a grey material with a patch of red sewn on its head. The scientist was using the puppet to feed the crane chick. The caption above the photo read: *Isolation Rearing*.

Tess skimmed the section quickly, then gave a loud whoop. She had found the solution she'd been looking for. Only two more rooms to vacuum and she'd be finished. She switched the vacuum back on and sang as she worked.

When she was finished, she put the book in her backpack, got on her bike, and rode over to Clara's. The bird woman was sitting on the porch painting when she arrived.

"Crane costumes," said Tess, breathlessly. "The researchers dressed up in them to fool the cranes. The downys thought they were their mothers. So the cranes didn't imprint on humans. Look, it's all here in the book."

She was so excited she couldn't sit still.

"I could sew them. The crane costumes ... for all of us!"

Clara didn't say a word. She didn't look excited. She wasn't even smiling.

Tess felt her face growing hot.

"You think it's impossible?" she asked.

"Anything's possible," said Clara kindly. "That's what's so wonderful about being young. You can dream big. And sometimes those dreams can come true. But so many things can go wrong, too."

"But I want to try," said Tess. "Tell me we have a chance."

Clara hesitated.

"It's a small one, but it's a chance."

"I'm going out to check on the egg. I'll be right back."

Tess *knew* things could go wrong. A raccoon or a coyote might break into the box and steal the egg. The bantam might shirk her duty. The egg might be infertile.

When Tess approached the box, the hen began to cluck excitedly. Tess opened the door and gently lifted the bantam from the box, placing her on the ground so she could feed. Then Tess examined the egg. It was beautiful. The pale mauve and green mottle looked like dawn light shining through the mist.

Thank goodness, there were no changes in colour or odour, signs of decay.

She turned the egg about forty-five degrees. Then she waited for the bantam to finish her food.

About ten minutes later, Tess sprinkled the egg with lukewarm water as Clara had instructed, placed the bantam back on the egg, and fastened the plastic door.

Returning to the cabin, she found Tabi waiting for her. The bird began to bugle, snuffle, flap his wings, and bounce. Then he made the contact call. Tess rolled her tongue in a long drawn-out purr. Tabi purred back.

"Dance with him, will you, Tess?" asked Clara. "My leg's pretty sore today."

So Tess hopped and twirled and bowed and purred. She used one hand as a beak and pretended to poke at the air. She used the other as a wing, waving it up and down. Tabi spun around her, stamping his feet and beating his wings in small stiff exaggerated arcs. Tess tried to mimic the crane's movements, ending each sequence with a deep bow.

"Bravo! Bravo!" said Clara, as she tried to clap and stand.

Suddenly, Tess heard a loud crash.

Clara was sitting on the floor, her crutches beneath her.

Tess bent over her. "Are you all right?" she asked.

"Still ticking," said Clara, struggling to her feet. "But I feel like a goose whose feathers have been clipped."

Tess helped her to a chair and propped her leg up on a footstool.

Clara sighed. "I'm used to being on the go, writing down sightings, locations, calls. That's what makes life interesting. Hammerfield's going to have a fit when he finds out I'm laid up. He's going to accuse me of getting old."

"Who's Hammerfield?" asked Tess.

"A birder from Wisconsin. An old rival. He keeps an eye on the greaters out there. We've been sharing crane data for twenty-five years."

Tess made Clara a pot of tea and a grilled cheese

sandwich. By the time Tess left, the bird woman had fallen fast asleep. Tess pulled a comforter from a cupboard and tucked her in.

"Sleep tight, Clara," whispered Tess, blowing her a kiss. Then she got on her bike and headed down Pitt Road to tell Sally the good news.

The Katzie reserve was about a half a mile off the main road. It was a small reserve, according to Sally, consisting of a cluster of thirty or more houses. The Pitt River ran past it. At the entrance of the river road there was a long dock jutting out into the river with about fifteen fishing boats moored there. A sign hung from a weathered beam. The sign read: *Katzie Landing.*

A couple of fishermen waved at her as she walked past.

Sally had said she lived in the second grey house on the river road. Tess saw the name "Pierre" on the mailbox.

A large black dog barked at her as Tess walked up the driveway.

"Stop that, Blackie," said an old man, bent over the hood of his car. He was wearing a pair of grease-stained coveralls and had a wrench in his hand. His long black hair was tied in a knot at the back.

"Is Sally home?" asked Tess, suddenly shy.

"Sally," called the old man. "You got company."

"Tess!" screamed Sally. "What are you doing here?"

Tess put a finger across her mouth, then whispered, "I've got something to tell you."

"Grandfather," said Sally, "this is Tess."

The old man nodded and continued to work on his car.
"Hi, Tess."

"Hi."

"Here, Tess, could you hold this wrench for me for a minute. This carburator is acting up like crazy."

Tess held the wrench, while the old man bent over the hood.

Suddenly he looked up. "Is this the crane girl?"

Sally giggled. "Yup."

Tess looked surprised.

"That's a compliment," said Sally. "Cranes are a powerful spirit for girls. Right, Grandfather?"

"Yes, my granddaughter."

Tess felt the old man's eyes meet hers. And in that moment, she knew he was someone she could trust.

She wanted to ask him more questions, but before she had time to say another word, Sally's grandfather went inside the house.

"Let's walk down by the river," said Sally. And Tess could tell by the way Sally took her arm that she was glad to see her.

At the end of the driveway, Sally asked, "What's up?"

"Crane costumes!" said Tess. "I want you to help me make them! We'll have to collect feathers. Lots of them. For the hands and the arms. And we'll have to make puppets, too."

· 18 ·

A Large Family

THE CRANES WERE flying away. Tess ran towards their nest and picked up an egg. It was rotten.

Tess awoke with a jolt from her dream. She glanced at the clock. It was four o'clock in the morning. A shaft of moonlight shone through the bedroom window.

She'd been having bad dreams ever since they'd taken the crane egg last week. What if the disturbance to the nest caused the crane pair to abandon it?

Tess lay in the darkness thinking. She felt frustrated. Neither Sally nor Zak could go with her to check the crane nest this weekend. Sally was going fishing and Zak had promised his mom he'd do chores. That left Tess, but she'd have to go on her own.

But why not?

"Why not!" she repeated aloud, surprised at the confidence in her own voice. Rubbing sleep from her eyes, she dressed, hung binoculars around her neck, and stuffed a sleeping bag, rubber groundsheet, flashlight and her notebook into her backpack. She was halfway out the door when she remembered Grandpa's watch.

She went back inside and tiptoed down the hall to her grandfather's study. Turning on the small desk lamp, she found the pocket watch in the top drawer, where she'd left it. She pressed the silver knob on top. The back of the watch flew open.

Inside the circumference of the watch, Tess noticed an engraved inscription. The script was so small that she had to squint to read it.

To E. from C.
With everlasting love
1945

Slowly it dawned on her. E. for Edwin. C. for Clara. Clara must have given Grandpa the watch! She must have been in love with him many years ago. But why didn't they marry? And why had Clara kept it a secret from her?

Grandpa's spotting scope lay across the top of the desk. Tess tied the legs of the scope onto an outer flap of her backpack and quickly dropped the watch into her pocket. The mystery of Clara and Grandpa would have to wait. If she didn't hurry, she'd never make it to the blind before dawn.

She stepped outside, breaking into a run, the spotting scope and backpack bobbing at her back. Crossing the back field, she slowed her pace, taking in her surroundings. Tonight the marsh seemed like a princess. She wore a dress of moonlight and a crown of stars.

Patches of cloud floated past the moon. Then the

shadows lengthened, casting shadowy arms from the trees and bushes.

Another howl. Closer this time.

From a cottonwood tree, a barn owl hissed. It swooped into the long grass, then flew away. In the underbrush, she heard soft rustlings. A hare or a snake? She'd never been bitten by a snake. There were probably lots of snakes hiding in the long grass, listening to her footsteps.

She imagined rows of tiny poison-tipped teeth. If she were bitten, they'd discover her dew-covered body in the morning.

Randall would say, "I knew she'd come to a bad end."

Years later, Rowena and Gail might say, "Remember that girl from the city? The one who died from snake bite." Then Tess's ghost would haunt the polder and scare them.

A harsh descending *keeeeer* sound broke the silence.

Tess froze.

Red-tail hawk. Unusual. Red-tails are late-risers. They seldom fly from their perches before ten.

Tess remembered the first time she had seen one. She and her grandfather had climbed the observation tower near Pitt Lake and they'd watched the hawk gliding in the updraft. In the sun, the bird's feathers looked a soft dusty rose. As the bird soared, its wings shimmered, changing colour with each slant of light.

"It's a talisman," her grandfather had said, as the hawk flew off.

"What's that?" she'd asked.

"A charm. Anytime you see a red-tail, good luck is sure to follow."

Tess hoped it was true.

The blind was about twenty metres away. Walking through the tall grass, she thought of the world about her feet — insects and small mammals sleeping, gathering food, burrowing, hiding — and she felt less alone.

Reaching the blind, she spread her groundsheet on the grass. She put her sleeping bag on top and curled up inside. She thought of the downy curled in its egg, its spindly legs tucked beneath its bony frame.

She cried out when the first clap of thunder hit. A downpour followed. She crawled under the groundsheet and watched the lightning zig-zag across the sky. Around her the marsh was lit with an eerie greenish glow.

One of Sally's stories, suddenly, came back to her. She'd said that when the thunder travelled through the sky, its power, the lightning snake, travelled with it. The lightning snake was a powerful Katzie spirit, but also a dangerous one. The creature had shining scales like a salmon and a sharp pointed nose that could penetrate trees. If the thunder grew too loud and rough, then the snake would become scared and flee. Sometimes the snake hid itself in the ground and sometimes in a tree, splitting the trunk down the middle with its pointed snout.

Tess hoped the lightning snake wouldn't visit her in the blind.

She was tempted to run back home. But she knew her grandfather would have said, "What's a little rain?" So she stayed.

❦

Tess awoke from her spot in the blind to the cry of a sandhill. The call was coming from the west. She grabbed her flashlight and pocket watch and shone the beam of light on the watch. Then she pulled out the small pencil from the side of her notebook and began to write.

May 31. The blind near Willowcreek Farm

1st crane call 4:50 a.m. 90 seconds in duration. Still dark outside, but rain has stopped. 2nd call 4:52 a.m. 70 seconds. 卌II 7 more calls, 70 — 90 seconds. 1 minute rest between calls.

It feels good to use Grandpa's watch. I thought it would be harder to time the calls, but it's just a matter of listening carefully.

Sunrise 5:11 a.m. – The sky is a clear deep blue. I can see the snow on the Golden Ears Mountains this morning. Set up spotting scope.

5:20 a.m. – 4 successive calls, 60 seconds in duration, 30 seconds rest between calls.

5:30 a.m. – I hear a high musical toya-toya-toya note. It's different than the usual garooo. It's the hen crane singing! She's sitting on the nest! I can't wait to tell Clara!

She'll say don't get your hopes up, but I can't help it. I'm so happy!

5:38 a.m. – A larger crane flew over the nest. It must be the male. It called out 4 loud garoooos, then landed in the hardhack.

5:42 a.m. – The male approached the nest and moments later, I heard the pair make the unison call. The female flew off, then landed about 10 metres from the nest. The parents changed places. The male turned the eggs with his bill, looking around every few minutes. Then he sat on the nest. The hen crane flew west towards Widgeon Creek.

6:45 a.m. – Male still sitting on the nest. Time to go home.

Tess out.

When Tess left the blind, she felt relieved and light. She'd been afraid, but she hadn't run away. And best of all, the eggs were still safe.

She remembered the moment when the female crane sang, the high sweet *toya-toya-toya*. The sound was like the slough tumbling over mossy stones or the willows waltzing with the wind. It was a melody she'd never forget.

All the way home she thought about birders round the world like her grandfather, Clara, and Hammersfield, who'd

spent their lives watching the cranes and sharing information. They were a large family of crane lovers. And that
morning, Tess took her place among them.

· 19 ·

A Notebook and a Pocket Watch

AFTER A QUICK BREAKFAST and a shower, Tess stuffed her notebook and the pocket watch into the front pouch of her jacket, zipped it up, and raced downstairs.

"I'm going to Clara's, Mom," yelled Tess. "I won't be long."

She left before Marjory could warn her about everything from slough water, to hyperthermia, to losing her way.

Along the ditches of Pitt Road, she noticed the hard white berries of the wild cranberries. This fall, she'd be here to watch the berries soften and ripen to a dark rich crimson.

She spotted a robin sitting on a fence post, then six more on the branches of a crabapple tree. She began counting more and more. On every branch and bush, she saw a robin! There were hundreds, no thousands of them! And then she remembered that the polder was situated along that great path of migration, the Pacific Flyway. Many of these birds were en route to other places, where they'd build nests and lay eggs in the spring. She made a mental note to write down her sighting in her notebook before the day was over.

As she neared Clara's cabin, she heard high pitched *goorahs.* It was Tabi. He began bugling and fanning the air with his wings.

"Settle down, Tabi," yelled Clara from inside.

"It's me, Clara. Hello, Tabi," said Tess. Tabi purred softly.

"Come in, Tess. Come in," shouted Clara, in a cheery voice. "You can let the ragamuffin in, too."

Tabi followed her into the cabin, snuffling and puttering until Tess started to giggle.

Clara was sitting on a chair, her cast propped up on a log. She was painting a black-capped chickadee in water colours.

Once the crane was inside, he began to snort and putter. Then he began to leap around the room.

"Now calm down, Tabi," scolded Clara, wagging her finger at the bird. "You'll give me a headache with all that commotion!"

Clara turned to Tess.

"He's excited because you're here."

"Really?" said Tess. Her heart fluttered as she looked at the tall skinny looking bird. "Hello, Tabi."

The crane walked towards her, spreading out his wings, as if drying them. Then he tucked his long legs beneath him and sat at her feet. Tess heard low putters of contentment rising from the crane's throat. He sounded like a car with engine trouble.

Tess remembered why she'd come.

She handed Clara her bird notebook. "Open it in the middle."

"What's this?"

Clara's eyes lit up as she read. "Second call 4:52 a.m. Seventy seconds. Seven calls, seventy to ninety seconds. One minute rest between calls .... The hen crane's sitting on the nest! You saw her!"

"Yes," said Tess, beaming.

"Wonderful. Wonderful. And you've recorded it all. You've even used birding language. Who helped you?"

Tess flushed. "No one. I did it by myself. I'll go again, too. Hammersfield doesn't have to know you've broken your ankle."

"Good for you!" said Clara. "Aren't you the brave one!"

Then Tess reached into her backpack and took out her grandfather's pocket watch.

Clara's eyebrows flew up in amazement.

"Let me see," she said.

Tess placed the watch in her hand.

Clara opened the clasp and read the inscription. Then she sighed.

"Were you and Grandpa ..."

"Sweethearts?" said Clara. "Yes. We were engaged for a time. Before Edwin met Mary, your grandmother. I'd thought of telling you more than once. But since Edwin hadn't, and I didn't know how you'd feel about it ..."

"I think it's romantic," said Tess.

"It was," said Clara, "but I broke off the engagement."

"Didn't you love him?"

"Yes I did. Very much. But I had to make a choice between art school and marrying Edwin. My father offered to send me to Paris for two years. I could attend one of the finest art schools in Europe — something I'd always dreamed of — or I could marry Edwin, become a farmer's wife, and lose my inheritance."

"But why didn't your father want you to marry Grandpa?"

"He wanted me to marry someone educated and rich."

"Grandpa was smart."

"Edwin was one of the smartest men I've ever met, but he didn't have schooling. He had to quit school when he was fourteen and help his father with the farm. He always found time to read though. He educated himself that way. Even in his twenties, he knew more than my father, who was a university man. But that's not what I saw in him ... He was one of the gentlest men I'd ever met ... and the kindest. And it took so little to make him happy." Clara's eyes suddenly filled with tears. "A bud opening, the birth of a downy, the sun rising between the Golden Ears Mountains — they were like miracles to him."

Clara pulled a tissue from her pocket, dabbed her eyes, and blew her nose.

Tess swallowed, fighting back her own tears. "But you chose Paris."

"Yes, and by the time I realized what a foolish choice I'd made, Edwin was engaged to your grandmother."

"Did Grandpa know how you felt?"

"No. It was too late. An engagement is a promise. He never would have broken it. After your grandmother passed away, I wanted to see him again, but I had too much pride. I thought I had time ..."

Clara smiled through her tears. "I have my art and that is another kind of love. But sometimes when I hear the cranes sing, I feel Edwin's presence."

"So do I," said Tess, and she gave Clara a hug.

"You know, I'm glad your Grandpa married Mary."

"But I thought ..."

"If he hadn't, my little chickadee, you wouldn't exist!"

"That's true!"

And they both laughed.

"Now I think this calls for a spot of tea," said Clara. "Would you mind, Tess?"

"Not at all," said Tess, putting on the kettle. "We can talk while we're waiting for the water to boil."

· 20 ·

A Fine Seam

JUNE WAS A MONTH of daisies, Queen Anne's lace, sweet clover, and lingering buttercups. The berry season in the polder was just beginning: salmonberry, fire cherry, and the hard green promise of blackberries which had just begun their long slow journey towards ripening in late August.

The crane egg was a week old. So far Tess hadn't noticed any discoloration on the shell. But she knew there was no way of knowing for sure.

Sally kept asking, "When are we going to make the crane costumes?"

"Let's wait," said Tess. "The incubation period is thirty days. So we have three weeks before the egg will hatch." Making the costumes seemed too hopeful. When a second week passed with no signs of decay, Tess decided to take a chance. But she didn't want her uncle to know. He'd laugh at her.

"We could sew the crane suits at my house," said Sally. "This weekend. You could stay for a sleepover."

Tess felt a pang of homesickness as she remembered the sleepovers at Martine's. They'd be up all night giggling.

Then in the morning they'd wander down the city streets, arm in arm, to The Coffee Bean to meet their friends.

"My grandmother said she'd give me her old sewing machine," continued Sally, "if I learn how to use it."

"You'll learn," said Tess.

Tess spent Friday night locked in her room. She cut out four crane patterns from newspaper and masking tape. It wasn't easy, but she'd watched her mother do it often enough. She made one pattern for herself and one for Sally, then a wider one for Clara, and a longer one for Zak.

"What are you up to?" called her mother, knocking on her door.

"Working," said Tess, which was true. She was too embarrassed to admit she was going to sew crane suits. Mom wouldn't laugh in front of her, but she might behind her back. And she had to admit, crane costumes sounded silly. She knew, also, that her mother would be surprised at her willingness to start sewing again.

She glanced at the worn grey sheets folded on her bed. Earlier in the week she'd taken them to Sally's mom who had dyed them grey. *Pearl grey.* That's how Grandpa used to say it — the colour of crane.

When Saturday morning arrived, Tess took over her sewing basket, the patterns and sheets to Sally's house.

"I'll cut out Zak's and Clara's," said Tess, "if you cut yours and mine."

Sally tried to steady her fingers when she cut out the

pattern.

"I'm afraid of making a mistake."

"It doesn't have to be perfect," said Tess. She was beginning to sound like her mother.

After they'd cut out the patterns, Tess showed Sally some sewing tricks, like rolling the thread between her thumb and forefinger to make a knot and licking the end of the thread so it was easier to poke through the needle's eye. Then she taught her stitches: an overhand stitch and a hem stitch.

When they'd pinned the sheets together, Sally sat in front of the sewing machine. It was an old-fashioned machine, nothing like her mother's, but in some ways it was simpler.

"Put the material under the pressure foot," instructed Tess. "Now put the pressure foot down. The foot treadle's on the floor. That's what makes the machine start sewing. Push on the treadle gently with your foot."

The machine made a loud clicking sound, like the hooves of hundreds of horses clattering down a city street.

"Help! It's sewing without me," said Sally.

Tess laughed. "Not too fast. Push the treadle gently. That's the way. Push the material through. Keep the seam straight. Good! That's the way! Now you've got it!"

Sally bent over the machine with a look of concentration, pushing the material through until she came to the end of the seam.

"That's a fine seam," said Tess. "You've got the knack."

"Wheee! I can sew!" said Sally, proudly.

It was fun teaching Sally how to sew, especially because Sally was so excited about learning. She herself had been a terrible student. Sally's eagerness made her own resistance more obvious. She felt a twinge of admiration for her mom's patience.

Tess surprised herself at the pleasure she felt in teaching Sally to sew. She sensed that it was a way of strengthening their friendship. Sewing could be a bond between them — a female bond — especially if you let yourself enjoy it. Maybe that's what her mother had wanted.

By the end of the afternoon, they had sewn four grey crane gowns and four hoods. They cut holes for the eyes and mouths.

"We have to sew the feathers by hand — along the hem and sleeves. That's going to take longer."

Sally dumped a sack of feathers on the table. "My brothers and sisters collected these."

"What kind are they?" asked Tess, sorting them into piles.

"Chicken, goose, gull, pigeon, and four eagle feathers. The eagle feathers are a gift from my grandfather," said Sally.

"They're beautiful," said Tess.

As Tess sewed on each feather, she imagined the chick curled up in the egg and the day when the baby would peck its way out of the shell. They sewed all day. As they stitched, they listened to the radio. And whenever they recognized a song they sang along.

"Where's your grandfather?" asked Tess. She wanted to thank him for the eagle feathers.

"He's at the smokehouse," said Sally.

"What does he do there?" asked Tess.

"If people are sick, he makes them better. My grandfather has special powers."

"What kind of powers?"

"He can heal people ... and he has a way of knowing things about people before they do. My grandfather teaches me lots of things ... because I've got big ears."

"Pull your hair back," giggled Tess. "Your ears aren't big."

"No. Big ears means I sit up and listen really well when he tells me things. I remember things, too."

❧

It was ten o'clock that night when they'd sewed the last feather on their crane suits. They were so tired they felt giddy.

"Let's try them on," said Tess, pulling on the long grey gown. She put on the hood and looked in the mirror. No part of her skin was visible.

Sally turned up the music on the radio. And suddenly,

Tess's body felt light and her arms felt like wings. She began to wave her arms and twirl round the room and Sally followed her. They danced like sandhill cranes, bowing and leaping and twirling until they were so dizzy they fell into a laughing heap.

When Sally pulled off her crane hood, she had a worried look on her face.

"What if the egg doesn't hatch?" she asked.

"I don't know," replied Tess.

Later, snuggled under Sally's quilt, they were too excited to sleep. They lay awake for hours talking.

Tess was dying to tell Clara's secret, but she decided it wasn't hers to tell. So she told Sally about her dad and his letters. Mom had showed them to her once and she'd never forgotten them. One of the letters began, "My darling Marjory." Another said, "Give my love to our sweet daughter, Tess."

"Your dad must have been nice," said Sally.

"My mother said he was. I've got a photograph of him and sometimes I try and imagine the man in the picture coming alive. But I can never quite imagine him. I wish I could see my dad, even for one minute. Then I'd have that memory for my whole life."

In the distance, Tess could hear a low drumming.

"What's that?" she asked, sitting up in bed.

"It's coming from the smokehouse," said Sally. "Sometimes the smokehouse people drum the whole night. But they do that more often in the winter, when they have their winter dances."

"How do you sleep through it?" asked Tess.

Sally laughed. "If you live on the reserve, you get used to it."

"Tell me a story," said Tess.

"I'll tell you a Swaneset story," said Sally. "Swaneset travelled to the country of the sockeye salmon people. These people were different from other beings because most of the year they were human. But in a certain season they changed into salmon and travelled in the sea.

"Swaneset met the daughter of the salmon people chief and married her. Later he brought his salmon wife home to Katzie. Soon after, Swaneset moved his home down river to Hammond Mill. Swaneset's wife showed the Katzie how to make twine from the long stalks of the nettle plant. Then she showed them how to make dip-nets with the twine. This meant the Katzie could catch the salmon wife's friends and relatives when they came to visit her. When the salmon wife bore Swaneset's first son, the river swarmed with sock-eye salmon. Up until this time, the Katzie hadn't known this kind of fish. When the people caught the salmon, Swaneset's wife showed the Katzie how to prepare and cook the fish without breaking the bones. Then she warned them to return the fish bones to the river.

"She said, 'If the bones of my people are lost or thrown away, my relatives will be unable to return to their human state. They will die.'"

"What if the people lost a bone by mistake?" asked Tess.

"The person might not be able to come alive. Or they might be crippled or sick in the head. So from that time on, the Katzie returned the salmon bones to the river. My grandfather and I still do it."

Tess thought for awhile.

"Do all the Katzie throw the bones back?" she asked.

Sally shook her head. "No. Many of them have forgotten. But my grandfather says it's good to remember the old ways."

And then, Tess's eyes felt heavy and the next thing she knew it was morning.

A Promise Fulfilled

THE NEXT MORNING, after breakfast, Tess thanked Sally and her mom for the sleepover. Then she left for home.

A mile down Pitt Road, she cut across a field on the Henderson property. It was a shortcut which led to the dyke road. The back road was a pretty route to Willowcreek Farm.

The sun was warm, so she tied her jacket around her waist. As she neared the dyke, she saw that the wild roses were in bloom.

The bushes were an explosion of delicate pink flowers, each blossom bursting with fragrance.

Grandpa loved wild roses. They both did. She took a deep breath and let the sweetness enter her lungs.

Cheerily cheer-up cheerio! Cheerily cheer-up cheerio! came the sound of a robin.

"Hello, robin," chirped Tess. The robin was sitting on a rose bush behind her. "Aren't the roses beautiful?" She stuck her head in blossom after blossom, smelling the rich scent.

Then a song, higher and louder than the robin's, filled the marsh.

Crane music.

Tess was taken aback. Cranes were seldom seen at midday. They were more likely to be seen at dawn or dusk. But it sounded exactly like a crane.

She climbed onto the dyke and searched the hardhack on the slough side of the dyke, looking for movement. But she saw nothing. She took out her binoculars and scanned the marsh grass and sedges growing along the slough banks. Something emerged from the bushes. Something large.

It was the cranes! She could see them clearly now.

Tess held her breath and began to count. One, two ... five ... six cranes, their wings spread open like silver capes. Slowly, she moved towards them, afraid to breathe. She was afraid she might frighten them away. She edged towards some sweet gale bushes, her heart beating wildly. Stationing herself behind the shrubs, she peered out. The cranes moved slowly, leaping as they whirled. With each leap, the birds seemed to gain momentum. They leaped higher and higher, their bent legs springing into the air with a flourish, until Tess imagined the cranes leaving the earth, their red crests bobbing over the clouds. When they landed, they lowered their heads and closed their wings, spinning around one another and stamping their feet.

The cranes were dancing! Tess felt a lump form in her throat and her eyes began to swim.

Suddenly, the largest crane raised one wing and dropped the other, and crane by crane, the wing-drop step caught on. After a time, the cranes began fanning the air with their wings, until a single crane broke step. The bird looked dizzy. He staggered a little, picked up a piece of marsh grass in his bill and threw it into the air. Then the crane stamped his feet and bowed deeply.

Toss and bow. Toss and bow. Soon the dancers in the crane troupe echoed the movements, adding startling leaps and graceful pirouettes. It looked like a cross between a ballet and a clown circus.

Then a small crane, an unmated single, began to sing. Its song sounded lonely and sad, like the cries of a little boy who wakes up scared in the middle of the night. After a time, the other cranes joined the lone singer.

Tess closed her eyes. She stood in silence, listening. And in the song she felt part of all the living things around her. That's when she knew Grandpa had joined her. The cranes had returned him. Back to the place he loved so much — the polder. His home — and hers.

Then the song changed — the sweet notes interrupted by a warning call. One by one the cranes flew off and Tess found herself alone.

I've seen the cranes dance, Grandpa.

Tears ran down Tess's cheeks. She felt a mixture of happiness and sadness, something for which she had no words.

· 22 ·

Family Secrets

W<small>HEN</small> T<small>ESS</small> <small>ARRIVED</small> home, she saw a black limo parked outside.

"Who's here, Mom?" asked Tess.

"Some business associates of your uncle's. He's entertaining them in the study. How was the sleepover?" asked her mother.

"It was fun."

Marjory looked at her curiously. "What's that sticking out of your backpack? It looks like your sewing basket."

"Huh, oh yeah. I guess it is," said Tess, sheepishly.

"You've been ... sewing?" teased her mom.

Tess flushed. "I showed Sally how."

"What did you make?" she asked.

Tess hesitated. She may as well confess. Her mother would probably find out anyway. She took a deep breath.

"Crane suits."

"Crane suits?"

"So when the crane chick hatches — if it does — it won't imprint on us."

"How do you know it will work?"

"I don't know for sure. But scientists have done it before. I read about it in one of Grandpa's books."

"That's amazing," said her mother. "It's hard to believe something so simple would work."

"That's what I thought, too."

"Let's see the suits!" said her mom.

Tess emptied her backpack. She spread the crane suits out on the table.

Marjory carefully examined them, then broke into a smile. "You did a wonderful job, Tess. I'm proud of you."

"Really?" said Tess.

"Of course," said her mom, and she gave Tess a hug.

Tess felt warm all over. The praise felt good, especially coming from her mom.

"Thank you," said Tess.

When she pulled away, she saw her mother's eyes were filled with tears.

"What's wrong?" asked Tess.

"Nothing really," said her mother trying to smile. "It's just ... it felt so good to hug you. It made me realize how much it's bothered me, the two of us not getting along. I've missed you." Her mother placed both hands on Tess's cheeks and kissed her forehead.

"It makes me realize how much I miss my own mother. We understood each other so well."

"Like Grandpa and I," said Tess.

"I suppose," said her mom.

Suddenly the French doors opened and two tall men dressed in dark suits walked up the hall. They were shaking her uncle's hand.

"Let's meet a couple more times before July twenty-sixth. If we can get our backers out, I'm confident we'll succeed. And if you're willing to sell, then it's more likely other farmers will follow suit. It's been a pleasure talking to you, Mr. De Boer."

The men gave Tess and her mother a brief nod, then left.

Randall went whistling into her Grandpa's study.

"Grandpa would have hated Uncle Randall's plans," said Tess.

Her mother's face hardened.

"You judge your uncle so harshly and you don't know the half of it."

"I don't know the half of it, because you've never told me!" The anger in Tess's voice surprised her and she shrank from it.

"Some things are better left unsaid," said her mother.

"I want to know about my grandmother."

Marjory's face turned white.

"Why?"

"No one ever mentions my grandmother. Not even Grandpa when he was alive. I know she died a few months before my first summer at Willowcreek. But that's all. It's as if she didn't exist."

"I suppose it's time you knew," sighed Marjory. She walked over to the window and stared outside. She didn't speak for a long time.

Then she said, "Your grandmother was strong in some ways, but she was fragile in others. I think we all spent our lives trying to please her. Especially your grandfather. My mother was a city girl, born in Amsterdam, Holland, and when your grandfather brought her here, she found country life difficult. My brother was born when I was three."

"Randall?"

"No," said Marjory, looking into Tess's eyes. "Hans. Hans was born five years before Randall."

Tess's mouth fell open.

Mom had two brothers?

"What happened to Hans?" asked Tess.

Her mother put her hand over her forehead. Her hands were trembling.

"He drowned."

"No one told me," said Tess, her voice trailing off.

"It was a forbidden topic when we were growing up. I knew, if I mentioned it, my mother would cry. We were always trying to make her laugh."

"How old was Hans ... when he died?"

"Three." Tess's mom clasped her hands tightly as she spoke. The lines across her brow deepened and sorrow entered her eyes. "My mother was napping, as she always did on Sunday afternoons, and while she was sleeping Hans climbed from his crib and went looking for my father. Hans must have seen him carrying his fishing rod. My father was supposed to have gone fishing, but when he heard the cranes singing, he went birding instead."

Marjory rubbed her forehead, as if trying to wipe the hurt away. Then her voice grew quieter. "My father found my brother's body in the shallow water of the slough. Nothing was ever the same after that. My mother never forgave my dad — or the cranes."

"But why?" asked Tess.

"She believed the cranes led my father from the slough that day. If my dad hadn't followed them, he could have saved Hans from drowning."

"Did Grandpa think that?"

"No," said her mom. "Your grandfather believed the cranes were singing because they sensed something terrible was going to happen. He believed they sang to comfort him."

Suddenly, Tess remembered her Grandpa's eyes whenever the cranes sang — all grey and watery, like a slough mist before the sun burned it away. He must have been thinking of Hans.

"After that," continued her mother, "my mother never left the house. She kept me inside, too, except for school. When Randall was born, two years later, my mother became even more protective. She taught me how to embroider, crochet, knit, and sew, like her mother and grandmother before her. My mother loved sewing best. Everything in this house — all the curtains, tablecloths, quilts, and doilies — all these finely crafted things — were made by my mother's hands." Marjory glanced at her daughter. "She taught me all she knew, as I've tried to teach you."

Tess's eyes fell upon the white linen tablecloth embroidered with forget-me-knots and the blue-and-white gingham chair cushions, hand-stitched by her grandmother. She knew her mother spoke the truth, but there was another truth, one still unexplained. Why had her mother and uncle rejected everything that Grandpa had stood for?

"But what about birding?" asked Tess. "Didn't Grandpa ever take you?"

"He did when I was young," said her mother. "But not after Hans died. My mother wouldn't let him. She always had an excuse. The weather was too cold or too hot or too rainy or she'd already made plans. When Randall was born, he became the son she'd lost, and she wouldn't let my brother out of her sight. Sometimes my father would insist I go walking with him along the dykes, but my mother would become hysterical. She was convinced that something terrible was going to happen to me. Of course, I never learned to swim, which made her fears worse. And Randall has never gone birding. Not once.

"Once I remembered her saying, 'I lost one child to this forsaken place. I won't lose another.' They had terrible rows about it. Eventually, my father gave up."

"Didn't you hate staying inside all the time?"

"I did at first. But later, I became as frightened as my mother."

"Is Uncle Randall afraid?"

Mom thought for a moment.

"I'm not sure," she said. "But if he was, he'd never admit it. When Randall grew older, he resented how Dad was always outside birding. He thought Dad didn't care about us, but I knew that wasn't true. Dad would have loved to have taken us with him, but he had no choice. My mother was frail physically, but she had a steel will. She controlled Dad with her fear."

Things were beginning to make sense now. Her uncle's ambivalent feelings towards Grandpa. Her mother's protectiveness towards Tess.

"I wish you wouldn't sell the farm," said Tess.

"I can't make up my mind," said Marjory. She stood up and looked out the window. "Sometimes I love this house. Everything inside is old and familiar. The clock over the sink and the wood stove and the rocking chair in the corner — it's all very comforting. But at other times I feel like a prisoner here ... when the mist hovers above the slough and the rain beats against the window and the cranes are calling across the marsh. Then I want to escape, just as Randall does."

Marjory motioned to Tess.

"Come and look," she said, pointing to the sun setting behind the mountains. Tess stood beside her and they watched the sun fill the marsh with a radiant light.

And Tess could tell by her mother's face that she, too, thought it was beautiful.

· 23 ·

Trouble

THE FIRST WEEK IN June was hot. As if on cue, the marsh suddenly burst into flower. The hardhack thickets were covered with mauve pink plumes. The Labrador tea and the water parsley were heavy with showy white blossoms. And in the bog, Tess found her first insect-eating plant of the season — a round-leaved sundew.

The kids wore cut-off jean shorts, short sleeved tee-shirts and sandals to school and everyone talked about the summer holidays on the bus ride home.

"Only three weeks to go," said Zak. "Time to play baseball and basketball and sleep in."

"Time to go fishing," said Sally.

"And birding," said Tess.

"I'm going to the city for a week," said Rowena. "And I'm having lots of sleepovers." Then she smiled at Tess.

"Hey, Zak," said Sally, "I have something for you."

"You do?" asked Zak.

Sally unbuckled her backpack and tucked her hand inside.

"Ta dah!" she said, pulling out a crane hand puppet.

"What do you think?"

"It's cute," said Zak, pulling the puppet over his hand. *"Garoooo!"* he shouted, in his best imitation of a crane call. Then he poked the puppet at Sally's face.

"I'll take it back if you keep doing that," warned Sally.

"Okay. Okay. Who made it for me, you or Tess?"

"We both did," said Sally. "Actually, we made four puppets last weekend, one for you and Clara and one each for Tess and I. It was fun."

Rowena glared at Sally, then got up from her seat and moved to the front of the bus. Gail followed.

"What's wrong with *her*?" asked Sally.

Zak shrugged. "I don't know. She's been moody lately."

Sally and Tess exchanged glances.

"Thanks for the puppet," said Zak. "I hope I get to use it."

"Look!" said Tess, pointing out the window. "It's an eagle. It's flying over the field. It's a young one."

"How can you tell?" asked Zak.

"By its head," answered Sally. "An immature eagle's head is brown. A mature's is white."

Tess spent the rest of the bus ride with her nose pressed against the glass. She counted three more eagles, two matures and one immature, before she got off at Clara's. Since the bird woman had injured her ankle, Tess would often ride on the school bus to the bird woman's mailbox, then walk up the road to her cabin. If their calculations were right, the crane chick was due to hatch in two weeks.

Tess found Clara sitting at her easel, her leg propped up on a chair. Tabi was stretched out beside her, his head under his wing. When Tess entered, the crane shook himself awake and bugled a greeting.

"Hello, Tabi, Tabi, Tabi," crooned Tess. "How's my bird?"

Tabi leaped into the air, stamped his feet and growled. Tess leaped and stamped and growled, too. Then she burst into laughter.

"Tabi, you should have been a comedian!"

Tess leaned over Clara's shoulder, gazing at Clara's painting. A pair of rufous hummingbirds were hovering over a bush covered with bright red flowers. Red currant bushes, thought Tess, a hummingbird's first spring treat.

"Hummingbirds are so pretty," said Tess. "How's your leg?"

"It's on the mend," said Clara. "I made my first trip down to the henhouse today. It took me a good ten minutes to walk there and I used my cane. But it feels good to be on my feet again."

Suddenly Tabi flapped his wings and half flying, half walking, rushed down the hallway.

"Someone's knocking," said Tess.

"We're in here," bellowed Clara, cleaning her paintbrush with a drop of oil and a cloth. There were splotches of green and red paint on her hands and a dab of yellow in her hair. "It's probably Zak. He's bringing over a girl from his class. She wanted to see the crane egg."

"Rowena?" asked Tess.

"Did I hear my name?" asked a voice from the doorway.

"Hi, Tess," said Zak. Rowena was hanging on to Zak's arm.

"Hi," said Tess, forcing a smile.

Rowena nodded politely.

Tess felt hurt because Zak hadn't spent much time with her lately. Between his guy friends and Rowena, it seemed he'd forgotten her.

But he *had* asked her about the crane egg most days and he *had* gone to Clara's to turn the egg, so she couldn't really be mad at him.

Zak introduced Rowena to Clara. He sounded nervous.

"Pleased to meet you," said Clara.

"*Grawk! Grawk!*" said Tabi.

"Who's my favourite crane?" said Tess.

Tabi leaped into the air, then twirled and bowed.

"I think it's Tabi!" said Tess.

Tabi croaked with excitement. He stepped towards Tess with his neck erect. He fanned the air with his wings, then lowered his head and spun around Tess, stamping his feet.

"Dance with him, Tess," said Zak, in a teasing voice.

"We'll dance later, Tabi," said Tess, glaring at Zak. *Not with Rowena watching.*

Tabi cocked his head to one side, and gave Tess a contact call.

"What a fickle bird you are," said Clara, pretending to be annoyed. "All this time I thought you loved only me."

"Here, crane, crane, crane," said Rowena. "Oh, he's such a cutie."

"Be careful," warned Clara. "His bill is sharp."

"I'm good with animals," said Rowena. She leaned over and petted Tabi's bald cap.

Tabi jerked his head round and nipped Rowena on the forearm.

"Ow," wailed Rowena.

A small pink welt appeared on her skin.

"Oh. It hurts."

"Shame on you, Tabi," said Clara. "Out you go."

Tess opened the door and Tabi shuffled outside in disgrace.

"Bring me my first aid kit, will you, Tess. It's in the cupboard." Clara put disinfectant and a Band-Aid on Rowena's arm.

"That crane's bad tempered," snapped Rowena.

Good for you, Tabi. I've been wanting to do that for a long time.

"Show me the egg, would you, Zak?" asked Rowena.

You're not interested in that egg. What a phony!

"Sure," said Zak. "How's your arm, Rowena?"

"It hurts."

"I can't understand it," said Zak. "Tabi doesn't usually bite."

Rowena scowled.

"I'm coming, too," said Tess. She followed them to the henhouse. She didn't trust that girl one bit.

When they neared the henhouse, the bantam began to squawk.

"She doesn't want us to take her off the egg," explained Zak.

Speaking softly to the bantam to calm her, Tess lifted the hen from the nest box.

"Time to eat little bantam," she said, as she placed the hen on the ground near her feeding tray.

"There's the crane egg," said Zak proudly.

Rowena stuck her head into the box.

"Oh ... I want to hold it," said Rowena.

Tess stepped forward.

"No. It's fragile."

Rowena's eyes narrowed.

"You said I could, Zak." Her voice was whiny.

"I promised her, Tess. Row's been really excited about coming here."

Why can't you see through her?

Tess dug her heel into the dirt. She looked up at Zak. His eyes were soft and pleading. Her reserve melted.

"Okay," she sighed.

Rowena picked up the egg and brought it close to one eye.

"Hmmm," she said.

Tess watched as the egg teetered between Rowena's thumb and forefinger. Tess clasped her hands together tightly, her knuckles white.

Stop that. You're playing with it like a toy.

She held her breath as she watched the egg roll slowly back and forth in Rowena's palm.

"Don't ..." said Tess, reaching for the egg.

"I won't hurt it," said Rowena, holding the egg.

In that instant, the bantam fluffed up her neck feathers and began to squawk. Rowena stepped backwards. The egg slipped from her fingers. Tess watched it falling. She reached down and caught the egg like a slow moving fly ball.

Tess's mouth fell open. She looked down at the egg. It had a crack in it.

"You broke it!" said Tess and she felt something break inside her.

"It was an accident. I didn't mean to. Really I didn't," said Rowena. She looked as though she were about to cry. "Zak, tell her it was an accident."

Zak looked stunned. He looked down at the egg, then up at Rowena. But he said nothing.

Angry words swarmed inside Tess's head like crows. She tried to call them to her, but they darted in and out of reach.

"Oh, poor chick, you've killed it!"

Rowena's eyes flashed hard and bright. Cowbird eyes.

"It wasn't my fault," said Rowena. "That stupid hen made me drop it. Zak saw what happened, didn't you."

"I saw what happened," said Zak.

"See," said Rowena, folding her arms. She looked satisfied, as if all that mattered was Zak's opinion.

"You were careless," said Zak.

"Well!" said Rowena. Then she stormed off.

"Good riddance," said Zak. "We just about drowned for that egg — all for nothing."

"You think it's no good?" asked Tess.

"It's got a crack in it."

Her heart sank at his words. It was *her* idea to take the crane egg. If the chick didn't survive, it was her fault. She felt a sick feeling in the pit of her stomach.

Then she felt Zak's hand on her shoulder. When she turned, he put his arms around her. Holding the egg in one hand, she lay her head against his chest and listened to his heart, and hers, beating in unison.

When she pulled away, she saw the sadness in Zak's eyes. The egg meant a lot to him, too.

"Let's take the egg to Clara and see what she thinks," said Zak.

"What about the hen?" asked Tess.

"That bantam's possessive. She'll sit on it again later."

Tess held the egg gingerly, taking each step slowly, without speaking, afraid that even the sound of their voices might damage it further.

"What happened?" asked Clara. "You look like you've seen a ghost."

Tess placed the egg in her hands. "Rowena dropped it." She wanted to add "on purpose," but she bit her tongue. She had no proof.

Clara's face fell.

"Is the chick going to die?" asked Tess.

"It's hard to say," said Clara, examining the egg. "The shock of the fall is as worrisome as the crack. It's a good thing you caught it. We'll have to wait and see. Better take the egg back to the bantam. The chick might be a hardy sort."

"I hope so," said Tess. Her steps felt heavy as she walked back to the henhouse. The bantam looked up expectantly and began to cluck. Tess placed the egg carefully on the straw and returned the bantam to the nest box. The hen sat on the egg, closed her eyes, and tucked her head under her wing. Clara was right. They'd just have to wait.

· 24 ·

Four Big "Birds"

THE NEXT DAY AT school, Sally and Rowena were suddenly sent to the principal's office. When they came back to class, Mrs. Mitchell said, "We've had enough trouble to last us till the summer holidays. If anyone in this class mentions the word 'egg' or 'crane,' they'll be serving detentions with Sally and Rowena."

So everyone pretended nothing had happened.

On the way home from school, Sally told Tess the whole story.

"It started when I walked into the washroom at recess. Rowena was in there, crying. Gail and the rest of her friends were patting her on the back like mother hens. Rowena said, 'Tess is trying to turn Zak against me, because she likes him. It wasn't my fault the egg broke. It was the dumb hen's fault. I couldn't sleep last night because of Tess. She's so mean to me.' Can you believe the nerve of her? So I said, 'Stop blaming, Tess. *You* dropped the egg, not Tess.' Then Rowena started yelling at me. We must have been pretty loud, because one of the teachers came running in and we both got sent to the office. And while we were waiting for the principal to talk to us, Rowena said under her breath, 'You'll be sorry.'"

"It's all my fault," said Tess.

"No, it's not. It's the price you pay for howling."

At first, Tess thought Sally meant Rowena's howling, then she realized Sally meant not being afraid.

The next time Tess checked the crane egg, she noticed that the colour was unchanged and the egg had no odour. Since the chick was due to hatch in twelve days, Tess felt new hope that the chick might survive.

After the fight in the washroom, everyone at school was talking about the crane egg. "Any sign yet?" they'd ask or "How big will the chick be?"

Tess felt a little sorry for Rowena, because she knew what it felt like to be left out.

One day at lunch, Rowena called Tess over. She looked nervous.

"I'm sorry about the crane egg," said Rowena. "If I had to do it over again, I would never have picked up that egg. I am not a chick killer!"

Rowena looked as though she meant it.

"Oh. Huh ... that's okay," said Tess.

"When is the chick supposed to hatch?"

"This Sunday."

"I hope it does," said Rowena. Then she surprised Tess. She gave her a hug.

Rowena hugging her? Nothing seemed stranger or more unexpected. She didn't know what to think.

When Tess walked into the farmhouse, Friday after school, the phone rang. It was Clara.

"The chick's been peeping in the shell!" said Clara.

"I'll be right over!" said Tess.

When she arrived at Clara's, Zak and Sally were peering into the bantam box. Clara was sitting in an old wooden lawn chair. The bantam was on the ground. It was running in frantic circles and squawking.

"Has it hatched yet?" asked Tess.

"No," whispered Sally. "Clara says the chick won't break through the egg sac for at least twenty-four hours."

"Twenty-four hours?"

Clara gave Tess a sympathetic look. "At least," she said.

"How long after that will it hatch?"

"Probably not till Sunday or even Monday."

Tess groaned. "Monday's a school day!"

Zak shook his head. "After all we went through ..."

"... it would be horrible to miss it," said Sally.

"It *might* be Sunday," said Clara, hopefully.

"*Peeep. Peeep. Peeep*," called the chick from inside the egg.

Tess felt a lump in her throat.

She stole a glance at Sally, then Zak. They had looks of amazement on their faces.

Clara was beaming.

"Talk to the chick," said Clara softly. "A crane mother would."

"Do you think it can hear us?" asked Tess.

"Of course," said Clara.

Tess drew in her breath and peeped.

"*Peep*," added Zak and Sally in unison.

"*Peeeep*!" answered the chick.

Everyone laughed.

"That chick sounds healthy," said Zak with an air of authority.

"Peeping develops strength in the chick," said Clara. "That's why the crane parents talk to the chick in the shell."

"Then I'd better talk to the little guy," said Zak.

"You mean peep," said Sally.

Zak knelt by the egg and peeped repeatedly in a silly voice. The chick answered, at first, then grew silent.

"You've worn the poor thing out," said Sally. "Besides, peeps should be done with sincerity."

Zak pretended to be hurt, then burst into laughter.

Before they left that Friday evening, they talked about the next day. Clara was determined to stay up all night to keep an eye on the chick. But she couldn't possibly stay awake two nights in a row. If they slept over at Clara's tomorrow night, each of them could take a shift. No one wanted to miss anything. Watching a crane chick hatch was a "once in a lifetime" opportunity. They just had to convince their parents.

Clara received phone calls. Promises were made. Negotiations were held. Permission was granted!

While her mother made sandwiches, Tess stuffed a sleeping bag, crane suit, and crane puppet into her backpack. Then Marjory drove her to Clara's.

"I hope your little chick lives," said her mom in the car.

"Me, too," said Tess. Then she gave her mother a quick hug and ran down the path to the henhouse.

The first thing she saw was Clara fast asleep in the lawn chair. The bantam was pecking at a small mound of grain near Clara's feet.

"Is Clara okay?" asked Tess.

Sally nodded. "She's just tired. She fell asleep shortly after Zak and I got here."

"How *is* our little chick?" asked Tess, pressing her face against the edge of the nest box.

Zak grinned. "It's been making progress."

Tess saw a small hole along the cracked part of the egg. It was about the size of a dime. She could hardly contain her excitement.

"I can see something moving inside the egg! It's the egg tooth."

"What's that?" asked Zak.

"It's a small cap on the end of the chick's beak. The beak's orange, but the cap is white. I read about it in one of Grandpa's books. The chick uses it to break open the shell."

Throughout the day, the chick chipped away furiously

at the shell, then it rested awhile and began again. The bantam wandered aimlessly around the henhouse. Tess felt sorry for her.

While they waited, they played card games, talked, and ate. It was fun, almost like a birthday celebration, and it was, in a way.

Saturday passed quickly. But by late afternoon Sunday, everyone was yawning.

"How much longer?" asked Zak for the millionth time.

"An hour or two maybe," said Clara. "But it's hard to tell."

"Let's put on the crane suits," said Sally, "so we'll be ready."

"Good idea, Sally," said Clara. "If the chick starts pecking in earnest, it could hatch pretty fast."

"Do you have mine, Tess?" asked Zak.

"Sally made yours," said Tess. "I made Clara's."

Sally handed Zak the neatly folded gown.

"Thanks, Sally," said Zak. "I didn't know you could sew."

"Tess taught me," said Sally proudly.

For the first time in her life, Tess was glad she could sew.

Zak held the crane suit up against himself.

"A perfect length," he said, smiling at Tess. "You're a good teacher."

Tess felt her cheeks redden.

"Help me on with mine, dears," said Clara.

Tess helped Clara to her feet, then handed her the crutches. "I'm getting muscles in my arms from these crutches," she joked. But Tess noticed how tired Clara looked.

Tess and Sally helped pull the gown over Clara's head.

"We can put the hood and wing mittens on later," said Tess.

Zak admired himself in the mirror.

"Cool," he said. "I like the feathers. But it's hard to believe that the chick will think the person in the crane suit is its mother."

"The scientists in the Platte were able to fool the crane chicks," said Tess.

"Yeah, but they were scientists," said Zak.

"We have to try," said Tess.

"It might work," Clara said slowly, "if we make sure the chick never sees any part of us. Not even our fingers."

"Or they'll end up like Tabi," said Sally. "That bird thinks he's more human than crane."

Grabbing her crutches, Clara hopped to the mirror.

"I look like Big Bird," she said, waving her arms. And they all laughed.

Two hours passed. The chick chipped away furiously at the shell. Then it rested for awhile and began again.

They decided that one person would watch the downy's progress, while the others waited in the cabin.

A half hour later, Zak came roaring back.

"Hurry! The downy's almost out."

Suddenly Tabi leapt up from where he'd been sleeping. He arched his neck stiffly, expanded his crown and marched stiff-legged outside.

"Settle down, Tabi," called out Clara.

But Tabi had caught their excitement. He knew something wonderful was about to happen. He fanned the air with his wings, performed a twirl and a bow, then he sprang into the air, circling the henhouse and singing.

"Soon you'll have company, Tabi," said Sally.

It was dusk as what looked like three large cranes scrambled, and one hobbled, to the bantam box.

Grrraw, grrrraw, whinnied Tabi, leaping at the creatures in the grey gowns.

"I think we've fooled Tabi," said Zak.

Tess leaned over the egg. Using her wing mitt she adjusted the crane hood so she could see through the eye holes better. The chick had chipped a line around the big end of the egg. Pushing its tiny head against the tip of the shell, the chick gave a series of sharp jerks, then rested. Finally, the top of the shell flipped open like a little door and the chick forced its head and neck out and looked around. For the next two hours, the chick slowly and painstakingly struggled to free itself. Then, the chick pressed its wings against the sides of the shell and with an enormous push, the shell split open.

"It's hatching!" cried Zak.

Tired and bedraggled, the tiny sandhill dragged itself from the blood-soaked blue-veined interior of the membrane, stepped from the half-shell, shook its damp body and flopped into the straw of the nest.

"Ohh," said Tess. She felt Zak's hand on her shoulder. She reached back and touched his hand, then smiled.

"It's a miracle," said Sally in a soft voice.

"Three dozen miracles," said Clara. "That little guy survived a dunking in the slough, a bantam foster mother, and a free fall."

"Come here, little one," whispered Tess.

The sandhill chick had large sharp claws and long spindly legs. It looked gangly and awkward. And whenever it tried to stand, it tumbled backwards into the straw.

"It's too weak to stand up," said Sally.

Sally held the downy while Clara examined it. Its body was tawny except for its mid-back, its rump, and the outer side of its wings, which were a rusty brown. Its widow's peak was rust and its legs, feet, and bill were a tawny colour.

"Is it a boy or a girl?" asked Zak.

"Too early to tell," said Clara.

"I bet it's a girl," said Tess.

"I'm sure it's a girl," said Sally. "At least, I hope it is, so the downy can have babies."

Clara winked, "Then until we know otherwise, we'll think of our downy as female!"

"Yeah!!" said Sally and Tess.

The bantam mother perched on the edge of the nest and guarded her oversized chick. Every so often, she pecked at the strange beings in crane suits.

Tess tucked her sleeve-covered hand under the crane chick. The downy snuggled into the crook of her arm.

Zak and Sally curled their wing mitts gently around the soft curve of her crown.

A lump came to Tess's throat. The sandhill was so beautiful. Her tawny down had already begun to dry in the air, leaving it soft and fluffy.

Suddenly, the sandhill raised her head and uttered a loud peep! They jumped back in surprise and began to laugh.

Sally whispered, "We're going to have to practise our crane calls."

"Graaawwwk," tried Zak, hamming it up.

"Garooo-a-a-a tuk-tuk-tuk," called Clara, in a voice that sounded exactly like a female crane.

"What will we name him?" asked Zak.

"Her, you mean," said Sally, frowning.

"Okay. Her."

"She has long skinny legs," said Sally.

"And soft down," said Tess.

"She wobbles when she tries to get up," said Zak.

Peeeeep, peeeep, peeeep, cried the baby crane loudly.

"And she peeps," said Tess.

"Wobbly?"

"Stilts?"

"Peeper?"

"I've got a better one," said Sally. Everyone turned and looked at her. "Miracle."

"It sounds hopeful," said Tess.

"And lucky," said Zak.

"Hello, Miracle," said Tess softly.

The chick gave a soft peep and rubbed her head against Tess's crane mitt.

At that moment everything in the world felt absolutely, positively right.

· 25 ·

Miracle

IN JULY, THE POLDER was warm and green. Bees flew from flower to flower, their bellies swollen with nectar. Morning glories with smooth white trumpets bloomed in the thickets along the sloughs. In the moist meadows among the marsh grass, Tess discovered rose-pink swamp laurel, yellow irises, and white bog orchids.

The blueberry fields were bursting with fruit. Flocks of hungry starlings gorged on the plump berries, while Uncle Randall alternated between sighs of acceptance and shaking his fist. "Greedy birds," he'd mutter.

Tess's mother laughed, "Randall's been saying that since he was a kid."

Now that school was out, Tess helped with the blueberry harvest. Mom hired the picking crews and when Zak and Sally applied for summer work, she gave them jobs. Tess was glad. Especially when Sally agreed to help her with the basket picking. Basket picking was the hardest job of all, so gruelling that it could only be done in the coolest part of the day. They pushed baskets on wheels between the bushes. Then they'd knock off the berries by shaking the bushes by hand or by using a stick to gently tap the stem. Only the smallest berries were picked in this way. The regular crews were assigned the easier bushes with the large plump berries. But Tess didn't mind. She and Sally could talk as they worked.

Marjory hired Zak as a dumper. Zak got to work inside the cleaning and sorting shed. He had to dump large buckets of berries into the wind machine. As the wind machine blew off the leaves and dirt, Marjory and Randall sorted through the berries on a conveyer belt. They placed green or imperfect berries in buckets hanging from trays. Later, Marjory used these berries to make wine.

During the hottest part of the day, Tess and Sally helped Zak in the shed. While Tess's mother made lunch, her uncle loaded flats of berries onto his truck and drove them to the co-op. Tess imagined the blueberries from the polder travelling all over the world.

Some mornings Tess got up before dawn to go birding. She took her binoculars and her notebook and began listing each species of bird as she saw it. The year before, her grandfather had recorded two-hundred-and-twenty-nine species in the marsh, writing his "best sightings" on a separate page. Some of Tess's best birds were a green-backed heron, Virginia rail, bittern, osprey, snow goose, and the greater sandhill crane.

Seeing such abundance, it was hard for Tess to believe that one day the wet meadows and the bogs might disappear

— and with them the birds.

She could no longer read the local newspaper without getting upset. Many of the editorials supported development. In response, Clara wrote a letter which was printed in the paper. Tess pinned Clara's letter on the wall of her bedroom.

Dear Editor:

I am against Western Development's proposal to develop the Pitt Polder. To build on a marsh, the developers would have to drain the land. This would lower the water table, permanently damaging the marsh's delicate ecosystem. Hundreds of species of birds, among them the rare greater sandhill cranes, would disappear because of loss of habitat. Golf courses are especially harmful to wetlands. The heavy use of pesticides used to create a weed-free grass carpet destroys plant life and animal habitat, and the use of fertilizers encourages the growth of plants that will crowd out native plants. I urge people who are against these developments to attend the upcoming rezoning meeting on July 26 and help defeat the proposal.

Clara Williams, Pitt Polder

It was a good letter, but Tess knew that Clara's voice was only one among a crowd of other voices, many who didn't care about the marsh.

It was only when Tess wore her crane suit that she stopped worrying. But taking care of a crane chick wasn't easy. The crane suit was hot. And it was hard to spoon feed the downy with a wing mitten in one hand and a hand puppet in the other. Tess felt all thumbs, and pushing even the smallest amount of egg white down the chick's tiny throat seemed almost impossible.

"She won't eat," groaned Tess.

When Tabi was a downy, Clara had fed him egg white for the first week, then pablum. Later, she'd introduced fruits and vegetables, then insects, frogs, and worms.

"Keep trying," chuckled Clara. "That chick's going to keep you hopping."

Clara was right. Miracle was a fussy eater. The chick would eat egg white one day, then she'd turn her bill up the next. And the chick refused to eat pablum. Instead, she liked to play with it. The chick would poke her bill into the cereal, then putter, sending gobs of the white mush on Tess's crane suit.

"Naughty bird!" scolded Tess, then she clapped her hand over her mouth. They'd agreed not to speak in front of the downy, but to use crane calls instead.

"Let's try baby food," said Zak. He had no better luck. The chick scooped the baby carrots off the spoon with her bill, tilted her head back so it slid down her throat, then she jerked her head forward, splattering the orange mush over her feathers.

By the end of the first week, hunger made Miracle less fussy, or, as Clara said, less finicky. The chick began eating a mixture of egg white and pablum with a spoonful of applesauce. At two weeks old, the chick ate raw apple and carrot and popcorn.

Between the henhouse and the cabin, they designated a crane suit area. No one was allowed past the garden fence without wearing a crane suit. It was too risky. Miracle might spot them and it wouldn't take long for a crane chick to imprint on a human.

Tess took Miracle for walks in the meadows behind the henhouse. The crane chick stuck to Tess's heels, pecking at the feathers hanging from the hem of her crane suit. Every so often the chick tried to bob and twirl on her long stilt-like legs, but she'd lose her balance, tumbling into the grass.

"Is that a dance?" asked Tess.

Clara chuckled.

"Well ... it's an attempt."

"I don't think dancing is her strong point," said Tess wryly.

After her exercise, the chick took a nap. She'd climb into Tess's lap and fall asleep in the arm fold of her crane suit. Tess felt like a mother.

When Miracle was two-and-a-half weeks old, Tess and Sally both dressed in their crane suits and went out to the henhouse. Until then, Miracle had only seen one crane-suit mother at a time.

At first, Miracle looked confused. The chick curled up in Sally's lap, then she switched to Tess's lap as if she couldn't decide which was her real mother. Then as if seeing a solution, the chick nestled between her foster mothers and promptly went to sleep.

Tess wondered if the chick could tell *who* was inside the crane suit. Or was the crane suit the chick's mother?

Secretly, Tess hoped that the crane chick loved *her*, not just the costume. Then she realized that being a good mother meant loving your baby, even if the baby didn't return your love.

Tabi, on the other hand, wasn't interested in parenting. When Tess placed Miracle near Tabi's wing, Tabi sprang to his feet, gave a quick little snuffle, and stalked off. In fact, since Miracle had hatched, Tabi was acting strangely. The crane pulled socks and underwear from Clara's clothesline and hid them under logs. He rooted in her flower garden. He performed elaborate crane dances four or five times a day — bounding, twirling, trumpeting, and throwing sticks into the air. He gave raucous concerts at five o'clock in the morning.

"That crane's out of control!" complained Clara, gritting her teeth.

And so was Miracle's appetite. The crane chick wouldn't stop peeping.

"That chick's starving," pronounced Clara one next day. "She needs worms, lots of them, and insects and frogs."

So Tess and Zak spent the afternoon digging worms in

Clara's garden. It was a hot day, so the earth was warm. Tess liked feeling the soil in her hands and the slough breeze in her hair.

"I noticed Rowena was talking to you the other day," said Zak as he scooped up a wiggling squirming creature into a pail. "She seems friendlier than usual."

Tess laughed. "Yes. She said she was sorry about dropping the egg." Tess scooped up two fat worms and watched them curl up together. "Poor things."

"Maybe you noticed ..." said Zak. "I don't hang around with her much any more."

Tess gave him a shy look. "Yeah. I noticed it."

"Aren't you going to ask why?"

"Huh, I guess so. Why?"

"Well, Rowena is pretty ... and she's popular. But I saw the look in her eye just before she dropped the egg ... I think she did it on purpose to get back at you. She also knew that egg meant a lot to me, but that didn't stop her. But then it made her look bad. That's what she was sorry about. Not about the egg."

Tess felt a knot in the pit of her stomach. Rowena had phoned her two nights ago and asked her over for a sleepover. She'd been surprised by the invitation, but flattered, too. She hadn't accepted yet and she hadn't mentioned it to Sally. She wondered if it would be wrong to accept.

"Let's feed some worms to Miracle," said Tess. "See if she likes them."

Anything to change the subject.

Tess and Zak put on their crane suits and carried the worms to the henhouse.

When they arrived, they spotted the bantam trying to brood the chick. Suddenly, Miracle, towering over her foster mother, seemed disinterested. So they returned the bantam to the henhouse.

Using crane puppets, they took turns trying to push worms down Miracle's bill. But sometimes the worms would wriggle out faster than they could push them in.

When Tess and Zak told Clara, the bird woman laughed.

"You'll have to break them up, like the mother crane does," she said.

"Cut up the worms?" asked Tess in disgust.

"If you don't," said Clara, "the downy will go hungry."

Clara brought out a cutting board and a paring knife. Holding the worm between her thumb and forefinger, she showed them how to cut the worm into small bill-size pieces.

Zak and Tess filled the pail with worm casserole, worm stew, and worm burgers.

It worked! Miracle gobbled up the delicacies, chirping happily for more. When the chick was full, she made a nest in the folds of Tess's crane suit. Zak placed his wing mitt around the chick's head and the chick gave a loud purr of contentment. Zak's eyes met Tess's and she could feel herself blushing inside the crane hood. There were some advantages to wearing a crane suit on a hot summer's day.

Sometimes, when Tess watched the chick sleeping, she wished that Miracle was tame. Then the chick would always stay with her — like Tabi stayed with Clara. Until she remembered that if Miracle was tame, she'd never join her own kind. She then took back her wish.

With each passing day, Miracle's appetite increased. At first, the chick gulped down sixty worms a day, then sixty became a hundred then a hundred-and-fifty. Not counting snacks of houseflies, moths, and spiders. And whenever she was hungry, the chick peeped to be fed.

"Maybe we gave her tapeworms!" joked Zak, and they began to wonder if it were true.

Then Sally suggested they get help. They could advertise for foster mothers, as long as people brought their own worms.

"What do you think, Clara?" asked Sally.

"Perhaps I'll finally get a night's sleep," she said.

They made phone calls to the kids in their class and Tess designed a poster. She tacked it up on the bulletin board at the Pitt Meadows grocery store. The poster read:

BECOME A FOSTER MOTHER
ISOLATION REARING OF A SANDHILL CRANE CHICK
CRANE SUITS PROVIDED
TRAINING IN FEEDING METHODS
ADMISSION: PAIL OF WORMS

Beneath the poster they wrote their names and phone numbers and waited.

Rowena called.

"Gail and I would love to help," she said. "My uncle owns the fish and tackle store in town. He orders worms by the box. I can get lots."

"Oh ... that sounds great," said Tess. She felt uneasy about it, but how could she say no. After all they had *asked* for help.

· 26 ·

Decisions

THE NEXT AFTERNOON, as Tess, Zak, and Sally were walking down the path to Clara's back garden, they heard a soft thrumming sound.

"Hummingbirds," said Tess.

And she was right. They were rufous hummers and they flew round Clara's head, their orange and green feathers glinting in the sun like sparks thrown from a bonfire.

But when the bird woman turned, Tess blinked in astonishment. One of the hummers was sipping nectar from Clara's lips. Then another bird took its turn and the first bird would fly away. It looked like the birds were lining up for kisses.

When the last hummer left, Tess asked, "How did you do it?"

Clara beamed slyly. "It's an old little trick. Take some plastic tubing, about the length of a straw, dip it into a bowl of sugar syrup, and suck the syrup up the tubing. Next, put the tubing between your lips. If the hummers are used to you, they'll sip from it. Then gradually shorten the tube or simply coat your lips with syrup."

"Would it work for us?" asked Sally.

"If you're patient," said Clara. "The hummers have to trust you and that takes time."

Like friendship.

Tabi let out a loud *garoo*. Then he leaped into Clara's flower garden and began rooting with his bill.

"Stop that, you crazy bird," said Clara waving her cane.

Tabi picked up an iris bulb in his bill and dropped the bulb — flower and stalk intact — at Tess's feet.

"Oh, Tabi, what's gotten into you?" asked Tess. "You know that's naughty."

"He's jealous of the downy," said Clara, retrieving the bulb. "He's trying to get your attention — saying it with flowers."

"I have some good news," said Tess. "I went birding this morning, in the blind. And guess what I saw!"

"Downys?" asked Clara.

"Yes. Two of them!"

"Lucky!" said Sally.

"Two wild downys. And I missed them," said Clara.

"The chicks were a little smaller than Miracle, but they're just as cute. They were swimming alongside the mother crane. You'd have loved it, Clara."

"That's the last straw!" said Clara. "I'm going birding and that's that. That doctor tries to coddle me too much. You can't keep an old bird caged up too long. It does more harm than good."

Tess smiled to herself. It was good to hear Clara talking like that. She sounded like her old self.

"How about tomorrow?" asked Tess.

"Deal," said Clara.

Tess went to lie on the grass at the other side of the garden, listening to the sounds of high summer: bees buzzing through the roses and peonies, crickets singing in the grass. In the distance, she could also hear the soft rustle of Clara's newspaper, the low voices of Zak and Sally as they played checkers in the shade.

Tabi spread his wings and lay on the grass beside Tess with his long skinny legs folded under him. Every so often, Tabi would whinny. Then he'd fall back to sleep again.

Tess could hear the low rhythmic purrs of contentment as Tabi napped. If only she could forget the rezoning meeting, she'd be content, too. Miracle was healthy, Tabi was here beside her. If only things could stay as they are.

Then she heard the slap of Clara's newspaper on the wooden lawn chair and the tap-tap of Clara's cane as the bird woman paced up and down the cobblestone path.

"I should know better than to read Grayson's column," said Clara. "Nothing, but nothing, gets me more riled!" The bird woman slumped back into the chair, flung open the paper and began reading out loud.

Western Development will probably be successful in persuading the mayor and council to rezone the Pitt

Polder. If this occurs, Pitt Meadows will receive an economic shot in the arm.

The expansion of Sandhill Resort will include a shopping mall, hotel, condominiums, marina, and a mega-theme park. The Pitt Polder will become a self-contained village which will result in millions of dollars of revenue to the area.

Experts, hired by Western, have given assurances that environmental impact on the lowlands will be minimal. Sewage will be treated before it is dumped into the Pitt River. The treated water will be clean enough to drink, says one of Western's officials ...

Clara grabbed her cane and began to pace up and down the garden path.

"Cutting down trees, draining the water, blacktopping a marsh, and for what? Entertainment."

Clara waved her cane in the air like a sword.

"We've got one week to get our people stirred up. That's not very long. The developers will be there with all their bells and whistles: charts, surveys, diagrams, slides, and fast-talking experts. And those guys know how to talk. They could talk a squirrel out of eating acorns!"

Our people, thought Tess. She supposed Clara meant the people who love trees and birds and wild flowers and the mossy scent of a marsh. But how many of these people would go to the meeting? And would they speak out?

"Uncle Randall's going," said Tess aloud. "He'll say that money's more important than a marsh."

"But you could set them straight," said Clara.

"Me?" said Tess.

"You could tell them," added Zak.

"Not me," said Tess and suddenly she felt very small. Her heart raced as she remembered how she stumbled over her words whenever she tried to express herself. They were like water drops sputtering off a frying pan, flying into the air with no force behind them.

She wanted her words to be a dusky rose, the colour of the red-tailed hawk's wing. Graceful and eloquent. Words that set people's hearts singing or made their hearts thump, because, suddenly, they saw things in a new way.

You spoke that way, Grandpa.

But she felt she never could.

Tabi was sitting at her feet now. Every so often, he'd look up at Tess and purr.

"Are you going to speak at the meeting, Clara?" asked Tess.

"Of course," said Clara, "though I'm not sure how many listeners I'll have. They think I'm crackers!"

Suddenly, Tabi let out a loud guttural squawk and sprang to his feet.

"It's Rowena," said Zak.

Rowena was standing at the corner of the house. She was holding a pail of worms as far away from herself as possible.

"Hi, Tess!" said Rowena, smiling. "I'm here to help."

Tess coloured when she saw her. She caught Sally's look of surprise.

Rowena said hello to everyone except Sally. She wouldn't speak to her or look at her.

"They're red wrigglers," said Rowena, thrusting the worms at Zak.

Zak hesitated for a moment, then took the pail from her.

"Where's Gail?" asked Zak.

"She chickened out," said Rowena. "She went swimming instead."

"The crane costume's on the table," said Zak.

"You can't be serious," said Rowena. "It's too hot."

"You have to wear it," said Zak, "or you can't feed her."

A sulky look crossed Rowena's face, but she quickly recovered. Smiling at Tess, she said, "My mom said you could come over to my house next weekend for a sleepover. Gail's coming, and Michelle and Mary. Call me when you know if you can come."

Then she grabbed the crane suit and went inside to change.

Of course, Rowena hadn't invited Sally.

Tess saw Sally blink, then look away. She said nothing, but Tess knew what she was thinking. Betrayal.

The invitation was tempting. Why couldn't she be friends with Rowena *and* Sally? Better a friend than an enemy, that's what her mother always said. Why should she have to choose?

Five minutes later, Rowena returned wearing the crane

costume. She was holding the hood in one hand and the puppet in the other.

"The gown's too long," she said. "I'll trip over it."

"That's Clara's suit," said Tess. "I'll pin it up for you, if you like."

"You're an angel, Tess," said Rowena, smiling.

Rowena chattered away happily as Tess pinned. Rowena was pretty, when she smiled. She could see what Zak saw in her now.

But from the corner of her eye, Tess saw Sally leaning against the tree. She looked small and sad.

Tess knew how she felt. She'd felt that way herself often enough.

"I'm ready!" sang Rowena, giving her gown a flourish.

"You have to chop your worms up first," said Zak, handing her a sharp knife. "You can do it in the shed."

Rowena's eyes narrowed. "You didn't tell me I had to do *that*."

"Those nice juicy wrigglers are too big," said Zak. "They could crawl back out of the chick's bill."

"Ewwww," said Rowena, staring down at the pail of wriggling worms. "Will you do it for me, Zak? Worms are so yucky."

Just like a cowbird.

Once Tess had watched a cowbird push three sparrow eggs from a nest. She found them smashed and bloody on the grass. Then the cowbird lay her own eggs in the sparrow's nest, and flew away, leaving the sparrow mother to raise the cowbird's babies.

Zak took the worm pail from Rowena.

"I'll do it," he said, but he looked annoyed.

"Thank you, Zak," said Rowena. "I'll watch."

Suddenly, Rowena fell backwards. She'd tripped over a branch hidden in the weeds.

Tabi leaped up, startled. He began to squawk, flapping his wings and stabbing at the air with his bill. The crane lunged at Rowena.

Rowena screamed. "Get that bird away from me!" She swung the worm pail at Tabi's legs, hitting them below his knee joints.

Tabi looked terrified, but dangerous.

Sally sprang to her feet. She stood between Rowena and Tabi. Staring Rowena in the eye, she said, "Put that pail down."

Clara ran towards Tabi and shooed the crane from the garden.

Rowena stood up. Her face was pale and her hands were shaking. She threw her worm pail down, and brushed herself off.

Tess heard Rowena's voice, barely above a whisper.

"Stupid Indian."

Tess's eyes flew to Rowena's face, but it was expressionless. Had she heard right?

Sally's face, white and crestfallen, gave Tess her answer.

"Sorry, Rowena," called Clara, from the backyard. "Don't know what's got into that bird. Too much excitement, I guess. I'm going to take him for a walk. Settle him down."

"Keep the worms," said Rowena. "I'm going home."

Then she turned to Tess, "Don't forget the sleepover."

Tess took a deep breath. She locked eyes with Rowena.

"I won't go without Sally. But there's something else. I didn't like what you said to Sally. It was cruel."

Rowena flushed.

"You must have heard wrong," she said in a tinkly voice. "Well, have to run."

After Rowena left, Sally turned to Tess. "Thanks," she said.

For the next hour, Zak and Sally stayed to talk. They talked about bullying and popularity and how some kids would go to any length to please their friends.

Sally said that one part of her had no respect for Rowena, but another part of her wanted to be accepted. Tess and Zak said they felt the same way.

Sally and Zak left together in the late afternoon. As soon as they were gone, Tess let Tabi back into the garden. He let out a loud ratchet and stamped his feet. Then he began to stab his bill at the air, whirling in circles.

He's still upset, thought Tess. So she sat on the grass and talked to Tabi until suppertime.

"Time to go, Tabi," said Tess. The crane began to cry

and snuffle in earnest. She blew him kisses and gave him the contact call, but nothing seemed to calm him.

"He knows you're leaving," said Clara.

"I have to go or I'll miss supper, Tabi," said Tess. "But I'll be back tomorrow. Promise."

Then Tess walked to the road and Tabi followed her. The crane made strange hollow sounds, like nothing she'd ever heard before.

"Goodbye, Tabi. Goodbye," said Tess. She felt a shiver run through her for the cries sounded like distant warnings.

And then she heard nothing, for the marsh wind died as suddenly as the crane's calling, and a silence fell over the polder.

· 27 ·

Syahaha'w

ON THE MORNING of July 22, exactly four days before the rezoning meeting, Tess and Sally were sitting in the kitchen of Willowcreek Farm making a poster.

"What do you think?" asked Tess, holding it up to Sally. It read:

SAVE OUR WETLANDS

LET'S NOT DRAIN THE MARSH FOR A THEME PARK
SAY NO TO THE REZONING APPLICATION
SAY YES TO THE ENDANGERED SANDHILL CRANES
ATTEND PITT MEADOWS COUNCIL MEETING
AT PITT POLDER HALL
JULY 26, 7:00 P.M.

"It looks pretty good," said Sally.

"I like the pictures of Tabi and Miracle," said Tess.

"Did you ask if you could come over for supper tonight?" asked Sally.

"Not yet. What did your grandfather want to talk to me about?" asked Tess.

Sally shrugged.

"Don't know. You'll have to ask him."

The door slammed and Tess heard her mom and Uncle Randall walk down the hallway.

"They weren't supposed to be back so soon," whispered Tess. "Let's roll up the poster."

But it was too late.

"What are you doing, girls?" asked Marjory. She leaned over their shoulder. "Nice job. Where are you going to put it?"

Sally looked at Tess.

"On the bulletin board at Pitt Meadows Grocery."

Randall strode in. He took one look at the poster and began to frown.

"Quite frankly, Marjory, I believe your daughter has been brainwashed by that bird woman. She's crazier than a hoot owl. And you, Tess De Boer, you are about to learn a lesson about progress. It stops for no one, especially not for little girls too big for their britches!"

"I'm not a little girl and you're wrong, Uncle Randall. It's not that way ... progress, I mean ..."

But Uncle Randall didn't stay to listen. He walked out of the room.

Words had failed her. Again.

She caught a look of sympathy in her mother's eyes, but that didn't help. She didn't want anyone's pity.

"Ask your mom," urged Sally. "About supper."

"Can I go to Sally's for supper?" asked Tess.

Mom hesitated, then drew in her breath.

"As long as you're not home too late," she said.

"If we go the back way, I'll show you the wild downys."

"Are they much smaller than Miracle?" asked Sally.

"Yes," said Tess. "Skinnier, too. The wild chicks don't have four foster mothers to serve them worm pie and worm casserole."

"And chopped worm delight and worm beetle stew and worm cookies with chopped flies."

❧

They found the dead chick near the blind. It was lying beneath a hardhack bush. Its feathers were caked with silt, its tiny beak open as if poised to sing. Tess held the baby crane in her hands.

"Poor chick," she said.

She kept hoping for a jerk of its head or a fluttering of a wing. But though the chick's body still felt warm, Tess knew it was dead.

They dug a hole in the mud with a rock, then covered the spot with wet leaves.

"Maybe the chick's brother or sister drove it away," said Tess. They knew the other chick was alive, because they'd seen it minutes before. The chick had been rooting near the nest, until the hen crane gave a warning call and her chick scurried under the mother's wing.

"Maybe," said Sally. "But the ducks and eagles have been dying, too."

"Really?"

Sally nodded. "My grandfather's worried. He says it's a bad sign."

Darkness had fallen by the time Sally led Tess to the slough behind her house. Just beyond a line of trees Tess could see a long swirl of smoke leaking from the bonfire and a bent form sitting on one of the logs placed around the pit. To one side of the fire pit, racks of salmon were drying.

"There's my grandfather," said Sally. "He's cleaning salmon."

Tess felt a little nervous, but she was curious, too. Why did Sally's grandfather want to see her?

The old man was wearing a bright red and black bomber jacket with the words "Katzie First Nation" on the back. He wore a single black braid and a baseball cap on his head.

"Hello, Sally," said the old man, without looking up.

"Hello, Grandfather. I've brought my friend Tess to you."

The old man nodded.

His face was darkly tanned and his skin wrinkled, but he looked wiry and strong.

"Perhaps your friend would like some tea," he said. "Sally, would you make some for us?"

"Sure, Grandfather. I'll be back in a few minutes, Tess."

For a moment, Tess felt like saying "come back," but something in the old man's eyes told her it would be okay.

"Do you like salmon?" he asked.

"It's my favourite fish."

"Mine, too. Not many left now. Not like the old days. In my grandfather's time, there were so many sockeye the Katzie used spears to fish."

The old man pulled a salmon from a large cooler filled with fish. Placing the fish on a large block of wood he used as a table, he picked up a long knife and slit the fish down the side and cleaned its insides out. Then he put the fish into a pail beside him. "I've been fishing all my life. It's hard to watch the fish disappear."

"It must be awful," said Tess.

The old man nodded, then turned to Tess.

"You found a dead crane."

"Yes. A chick. But we just found it. How did you know?"

The old man didn't answer.

"Lots of birds dying around here. Eagles, mostly, but ducks too. It's a shame."

"What do you think's causing it?" asked Tess.

"Maybe pesticides. Maybe pollution in the river. Fifteen years ago, half the cranes around here died. A farmer was spraying his crops from an airplane. The government men told him, use another pesticide. So the farmer did." The old man shrugged. "One poison's as bad as the other."

"Sally said you wanted to talk to me."

"Yes, because of my dream. I dreamed this dream three times. Khaals, the Great Transformer, is in my dream and the two crane sisters. One of the young girls has my granddaughter's face. The other girl I did not recognize at first. The girls are gathering *wapato* in the slough. They dance on their toes, they laugh, they hold each other up. The Transformer approaches them and asks, 'Is that how you spend your days?' The two girls say, 'Yes.'

"So Khaals says, 'Fly then.' And the Great Transformer changes the girls into birds. Their arms become wings and feathers, their legs become scrawny sticks and claws, and their mouths become bills — until everything human about them disappears. And all that is left are two sandhills dancing in the mud. Then the cranes fly away. That is the end of my dream."

The old man stared into Tess's eyes.

"You were the other crane sister in my dream."

Tess swallowed hard.

"I was?"

"Yes," said the old man, his eyes glinting in the firelight. "When a human who has acquired a guardian spirit dies, the spirit must seek a new home. The spirit usually chooses a grandchild. It is usually a person who has suffered much, for it is suffering that arouses the pity of He Who Dwells Above. My granddaughter has suffered. It is hard being an

Indian in a white world. But I see from your eyes that you, too, know sadness. Perhaps that's why the two of you were honoured. Your guardian spirit is called *syahaha'w*. It means 'superior in everything.' It is the spirit of the crane."

Tess was too surprised to speak. She felt a shiver in her body as she sensed the truth in the old man's words. But she had no words in response. The language she searched for would not be found in books or conversation. It was the language of the spirit and she felt in awe.

"You look worried, friend of my granddaughter," said the old man. "You mustn't worry. The crane is a powerful spirit for girls."

Tess sat beside the old man, watching the sparks in the fire fly off into the darkness. The old man stared into his lap as if he were daydreaming. Neither of them spoke for a long time.

Then Tess asked, "Where is my guardian spirit, my *syahaha'w*, now?"

"Within you," replied the old man.

Struggling to understand, Tess tried again. "But how do I find it?"

"Do not try. It will make itself known to you when you need it and least expect it."

Tess looked up to see Sally and her mother walking towards them. Sally was carrying a tray with a teapot and cups. Her mother carried a large ball of dough and some wooden sticks on a wooden board.

"This should hold you two over till the salmon's baked," said Sally's mom.

"Bannock for Tess!" said Sally. "We'll bake it Indian-style over the fire."

"What's bannock?" asked Tess.

"It's a kind of bread, baked on a stick," said Sally.

Sally handed Tess a handful of raw dough and showed her how to wrap it lengthwise around a long stick.

"Hold it over the fire like this. It tastes delicious."

Tess held the bannock over the fire and watched the dough slowly brown.

"Smells good," said Tess.

"Did you have a nice chat?" asked Sally's mother.

"Oh, yes, of course," replied Tess, looking for the old man. But he had already disappeared into the darkness.

· 28 ·

Missing!

THE MORNING OF THE rezoning meeting, Tess glanced at her clock. It was already eight-fifteen. She'd intended to get up earlier.

She glanced at her list of things to do on the table beside her bed: phone the kids in her class to remind them of the meeting, get two more pages of signatures on the petition, put up two more posters, dig worms and feed Miracle.

She scrambled out of bed, showered, and dressed. Then she ran downstairs to the kitchen to make a quick break-fast. She had just poured some milk on a bowl of corn flakes, when the phone rang.

"Tabi's missing," said Clara in a small, far away voice.

Tess sat down. "How long?" she asked.

"Since yesterday," said Clara. "I've looked everywhere — as much as I could with this old leg. I've called and called. I was sure he'd show up this morning, but he didn't."

Tess felt as if someone had placed an icy hand on her shoulder. Tabi had wandered off before, but never overnight, and never for this long.

"I'll go out and look for him."

"Thanks, Tess. I've got to dig more worms. Miracle's crying with hunger. I'll go searching again, once our baby is asleep. If Tabi shows up, I'll send Zak or Sally out to find you."

Tess grabbed an over-sized fleece-lined sweater, wrote a quick note to her mother, and set out across the back field.

Though the day was sunny, Tess felt cold. Shivering, she tucked her hands inside her sleeves to warm them. She searched the hardhack first. Then she scanned the surrounding fields with her binoculars.

What if the crane had gone looking for her and had somehow gotten lost? Then she remembered the feeling she'd had in her stomach the last time she'd seen Tabi. Had she sensed then that Tabi was in danger? Or had Tabi known?

She pushed away such gloomy thoughts. She needed a clear head.

Tess walked along the dyke roads, cutting through farm yards, climbing fences, calling Tabi's name. She talked to farmers and their wives and a couple of kids from school.

"Tabi's missing. If you see him, phone Clara."

By midday, the air was muggy, a sign of rain ahead. As Tess walked through the fields, the dry grass made a sharp snapping sound and thistles scratched her legs.

There were few birds in sight at this time of day. Most of them had found shelter in the coolness of the trees. They would return later when the temperature had cooled. Maybe Tabi was sleeping in a hardhack bush, ignoring her calls.

No. If Tabi heard her calling him, he would answer. She was sure of it.

She tried to calm herself by naming the wild flowers as she saw them in her search. *Hawkweed, cinquefoil, goldenrod* ... She'd always done that with Grandpa and now she could feel him walking alongside her, naming the flowers, too. *Hardhack, fireweed, loosestrife, foxglove* ...

It helped to shut out the tired feeling in her feet, the lump in her throat, the uncertainty of what to do.

By late afternoon, she'd walked at least twenty kilometres. Hot and thirsty, she picked handfuls of plump salmonberries and stuffed them into her mouth. Then she sat on the grass to rest.

In the eastern sky, she saw storm clouds gathering. They looked like crows with huge black wings and open mouths.

An hour later, a dry wind began to blow. It raced through the fields and shook the cattails and the sedges and the willow branches. The branches made a clacking sound like skeletons dancing.

Tess put on her sweater, as the summer temperatures plunged.

"Tabi. Tabi," she called, but the wind snatched her words as quickly as she uttered them. Hoarse from shouting, she continued her search in silence, growing more discouraged with the fading light.

She felt drops of rain on her face, but she didn't mind. The rain felt good after the day's heat.

She checked her watch. It was five-thirty. Only an hour-and-a-half before the meeting.

Tess had walked through every dyke, farmyard, and field from Willowcreek to Clara's property. Now she stood a stone's throw away from Clara's cabin. She saw that the door was closed. If Clara was home, the door would be open.

That meant Tabi hadn't been found.

As she walked towards the cabin, she surprised a flock of savannah sparrows from a sweet gale bush. *Tswi-tswi-tswi*, they trilled.

From the shadows of the bush, about fifteen metres away, she saw two gleaming eyes.

It was a coyote. The animal must have been watching her.

Tess froze, then she met the coyote's gaze. The coyote studied her. He tilted his head to one side, then sat down on his haunches.

Tess drew in her breath and moved slowly towards him. For the first time, she wasn't afraid. The coyote looked curious, not fierce.

Tess talked to him in a soft voice. "Hello, coyote. I'm not afraid of you. You knew my grandfather. He wasn't afraid of you, either. My grandfather and I, we're birds of a feather."

Pausing to measure her courage, Tess continued to inch her way towards the animal. She saw the coyote's nose twitch. Then he turned his head into the wind and loped across the field. Halfway across, the coyote stopped and gazed at her. The coyote wanted her to follow him. Was he trying to help or playing a trick on her?

Tess followed the coyote across Pitt Road to the edge of Sandhill Resort. Then the coyote leapt across the slough ditch and disappeared into the bushes.

Standing at the side of the road, Tess looked down at the marshy water of the ditch. Though most of the hard-hack had been cut back, it was still a good place for a crane to root. The ditch was filled with insects, frogs, and worms.

She checked her watch again. It was six o'clock and the Pitt Polder Hall was at least a half hour's walk from where she was standing. She decided to walk towards the hall, checking the ditches on her way.

She felt her spirits sinking as the long straight road stretched out before her. There were no cars in sight. Nothing but grey clouds, grey road, grey light.

Oh, Grandpa, I wish you were here.

· 29 ·

Found

TABI WAS LYING in the grass beside the cornfield, his head tucked under one wing. At first Tess thought he was sleeping. But the crane was too still. Only his wing feathers fluttered in the wind.

Tess turned the crane over gently. The crane's stilt-like legs remained stiff, though his body was limp. But there were no signs of injury. She knelt beside the bird and stroked his feathers. They were wet, but they felt smooth as velvet.

She lay down in the cornfield beside the bird, wrapping her arm around the crane's breastbone. She placed her ear over the crane's breast, hoping to hear his heartbeat. But she heard only her own.

"I love you, Tabi," she whispered. "You're the best bird in the world. You're loyal and affectionate and funny. And you're a wonderful dancer."

She felt the rain falling on her hair and her face and on the great bird beside her. Since Tabi belonged to the wetlands, the rain seemed fitting.

Until this year, she'd always believed that the world

made sense, but Grandpa's death, and now Tabi's, was beyond her understanding. Tabi was only fifteen. Young by crane standards.

She remembered how Tabi liked to sleep at her feet, his head tucked under his wing. She remembered how he purred when he saw her and how they danced together on sunny afternoons, leaping throught the long grass, the blend of Tabi's whoops and her own laughter, their unison song. She remembered how she "flew" with him and how pleased he was each time he rose into the air.

Now you are flying in heaven.

She had cried little since her grandfather's death, but now something broke loose from her. She cried and cried, until she had no more tears. She lay in the field in a kind of sleep.

When she opened her eyes, the air was cooler. The sun had sunk lower in the western sky. The light was luminescent, the kind she'd seen during rainbows. But there was no rainbow in sight.

Tess brushed herself off, kissed her fingertips and placed them on the crane's bill. She felt something smooth and powdery on her fingers.

She brought her fingers to her nose. The powder smelled strange, medicinal.

No. It couldn't be.

Her fingers shook. She swallowed hard, then pried open the crane's bill wider, running a finger along the crane's lower jaw. She felt several small white pellets, lodged between the jaw's serrated edges. Probing with her fingers, she found two more pellets.

Pesticides! Tabi had been poisoned.

Anger rushed through her body. It began as a hard knot in her gut, then rose into her throat. The howl of sorrow which came roaring out scared her. It sounded like a stranger's voice. She slammed her fist into the mud, she cried and pounded the ground until her arms ached.

Worn out, Tess placed the pellets in her pocket and picked up the crane's body.

"I'm taking you home, Tabi," she said.

She walked slowly and awkwardly, cradling the sandhill's long graceful neck. She felt the ringed bones of the bird's throat, the place where his song rose. The weight of the crane's body was like the weight of her sorrow — heavy and silent.

As she walked along the dyke road, she saw someone walking towards her. It was Clara.

What would she say? Tabi was Clara's family.

"Is that you, Tess?" called Clara.

The bird woman looked like a wounded owl as she hopped towards Tess, her cane poking the ground with each step. Every so often, she stopped to rest, leaning on her cane.

"Yes, it's me," said Tess, suddenly glad for Clara's nearsightedness, glad for that extra few minutes before Clara's eyes would blink at the sight of the dead bird.

"Thank goodness I found you," said Clara. "Your mother's been worried sick. I told her I'd take you to the meeting. She's there with your uncle."

Then suddenly, Clara's gait changed. The bird woman half ran, half stumbled towards Tess.

"You found Tabi! Is he all right?"

Tess shook her head, squeezing back tears.

The bird woman crumbled to the ground. Tess knelt beside her and placed the bird in the old woman's arms.

"I'm so sorry."

Clara stroked Tabi's red cap.

Tess put her arms around Clara. But the old woman said nothing.

After a time, Clara asked, "Where did you find him?"

"In the cornfield by Sandhill Resort."

The bird woman examined the crane's body, running her fingers over the long neck, under the wing feathers, along the slender legs.

"No broken bones," she said. "No signs of a predator attack."

"I think he was poisoned," said Tess. She reached into her pocket and lay the pellets in Clara's hand. "I found these in Tabi's bill."

Clara stiffened. She rolled a pellet between her fingers, placed it to her nose, then brought it to her tongue. Gingerly, she tasted it, then made a face.

"It's pesticide. Undissolved pellets," she said in a flat

voice. "Tabi must have been rooting near the drainage ditch. He ingested a lethal dose."

Still holding the bird, Clara tried to stand up, but her cane slipped and she stumbled. She looked old and frail, as if someone had drained all the life from her.

Tess helped her to her feet.

"Are you okay?"

Clara nodded.

"I'll carry Tabi," said Tess.

"I'm going home, dear," sighed Clara. "I'm so tired. Tomorrow I'm going to bury him under the willow tree at the back of the house. It's a good place for a crane. It's wet there and has a view of the marsh."

"Clara?"

"Yes?"

"Aren't you going to speak at the meeting?"

Clara stopped, leaned on her cane. Her face was drawn, pale, the lines across her cheeks and under her eyes seemed etched more deeply than Tess had seen before.

"I've no fight left," replied Clara, her voice breaking.

Tess watched her as she walked away towards her house. Suddenly the old woman turned.

"Let Tabi speak," she said to Tess.

· *30* ·

Crane Testimony

TESS CARRIED TABI across the parking lot of the Pitt Polder Hall. The lot was full, which meant the meeting was still in progress. She glanced through the door of the brightly lit hall, then hurried to the side of the building. Safe in the shadows, she placed Tabi down on the grass. She leaned against the building, closed her eyes, trying to calm herself, but the same thought kept repeating itself.

What am I doing here?

She caught snatches of conversation. "... sewage into the Pitt River well within the guidelines of the ministry of environment ... water expert ... dumping a maximum of one hundred cubic metres per day."

Loud clapping.

Gathering her courage, she peered in the window.

It was like watching a movie from the darkness of a theatre. The mayor sat at a long wooden table, facing the audience. Two women and four men sat beside him — probably councillors. Their faces were stern. In a centre aisle, she saw a line of people waiting to speak at the microphone. Uncle Randall was third.

Tess spotted her mom first, then Sally sitting with her grandfather and her mother and father.

Zak was sitting at the back. Rowena was beside him. She was whispering in his ear.

Tess felt a pang of hurt. But she let it go. Compared with Tabi's death, those things seemed less important.

Sandhill's public relations man stepped up to the microphone. He was wearing a bright blue suit, a red tie, and a button with a picture of a sandhill crane. The man's teeth were even and white, and he spoke with a syrupy voice. He never stopped smiling.

He kept repeating: "... Marshland theme park ... world class golf courses ... tourist dollars ... exotic rides, restaurants, shopping mall, roads, hotels, condos ... tax dollars, jobs ... multi-million dollar deal ... luxury accommodation and first-class entertainment ... minimal environmental impact ... hundreds of thousands of tourists ..."

After the company man's presentation, many people cheered. Tess broke out in a cold sweat. It didn't sound good.

But her spirits rose when she saw Sally's aunt, chief of the Katzie, stepped up to the microphone.

The chief spoke quietly, but Tess could hear the anger in her voice. She said, "The Pitt Valley is a sacred but troubled place. The birds and fish are dying. The air and water are polluted."

When the chief finished speaking, a silence filled the room and only a few people clapped.

People didn't like what the chief said. They wanted to hear that everything was fine. Hearing another point of view meant making tough choices, sacrificing the short term for the long term.

"Cut the malarkey, chief!" yelled a heckler. "The polder's a swamp! That land's sitting there doing nothing. We should be grateful to Western Development! They're going to build up the area into something beautiful!"

Sally stood up. She glared at the heckler.

"The polder is beautiful now! Development will destroy it." Sally waved the petition. "Sign our petition and defeat Phase B!"

Good for you, Sally.

"Shut up, kid!" yelled the heckler.

"Order!" said the mayor, pounding his gavel.

Randall stepped up to the microphone.

"Ladies and gentlemen, Mr. Mayor and council. I sit here in disbelief listening to the chief's words." Uncle Randall puffed up his chest and spoke in a very loud voice. "Because a few birds have died, we're supposed to stop a million dollar project? Come! Come! Let us use common sense — though it's not very common."

Her uncle chuckled at his joke, then cleared his throat.

"Animals die all the time. For lots of reasons. If the chief's going to blame pesticides or pollution on the death of a few birds, let her prove it! "

Tess looked down at Tabi. Proof? She *had* proof!

She heard her heart beating loudly. Then the beating grew louder and more insistent, until it seemed to spread through her body. The sensation was like a harpstring gently plucked, so the waves spread through each limb. Her arms seemed to grow longer and lighter and her legs felt like long skinny sticks. And the song that rose within her was the sweetest she'd ever heard — sweeter than the first snowdrops in the spring or the marsh marigolds in summer, but sad, too. As sad as the cry of the loon or Willowcreek without her Grandpa.

Then something seemed to pull her forward, a kind of magical courage she'd never felt before.

She picked up Tabi in her arms and began to carry him down the aisle to the front of the hall.

As she walked, she felt lightheaded and buoyant. She felt as if she and Tabi were one.

People stared at her and pointed.

"Who is she?"

"What's she carrying?"

"It's a crane."

"Is it dead?"

"Aw!"

Halfway down the aisle, Tess glanced at her uncle. She saw his mouth drop in surprise.

Tess moved to the microphone. A silence fell over the room.

She stared into a sea of faces.

"My uncle said development does no harm," said Tess in a shaky voice. "He says he needs proof." She held up the crane's limp body. "Here's proof."

Everyone began talking at once.

"Quiet," said the mayor, pounding his gavel. "Will the meeting come to order, please?"

Amid the noise and confusion, the company man hurried to the microphone. The man patted Tess on the shoulder.

"While we all sympathize with the death of any animal, particularly the death of such a magnificent bird — and we don't wish to minimize the distress that a sensitive young lady such as this would suffer — ladies and gentlemen, this bird could have died of old age, sickness."

"Now, my dear," said the man, pulling the microphone away from Tess.

"Pesticide poisoning," added Tess.

"Beliefs don't constitute facts. Facts require evidence." He took a handkerchief from his breast pocket and began wiping his forehead.

Tess turned to the mayor. "I found these pellets in Tabi's bill." She took the pesticide pellets from her pockets and held them up.

"How much more proof do you need?" shouted a woman at the back.

"If this council wants to get back into office, you guys better listen to the kid," yelled a man in the front row.

People got up from their seats to get a closer look. They crowded around the bird. Two ladies began stroking Tabi's feathers.

"Order! Order!" said the mayor.

The mayor banged his hammer on the table.

"Mr. Walker, take your seat! I would like to ask this young lady some more questions."

"What is your name, dear?"

"Tess De Boer."

"Tell me, Tess, why should we listen to a young girl?"

"I'm not sure," said Tess. "But I hope you will. My grandfather loved the polder. And I ... I love it, too, because he helped me to see how special it was. Tabi was born in the polder and he died there. He died of pesticide poisoning. If Phase B passes, people will use more pesticides and they'll drain the water. And more birds will die. The ducks and eagles are already dying and there are only nine pair of cranes left. The polder's special. I hope that you defeat Phase B and preserve this special place."

She heard loud clapping and cheering.

"Surely, Mr. Mayor, you're not going to take the word of a child on a matter as important as this!" said Randall.

"Why not, Randall?" asked Marjory, standing up. The crowd turned and stared.

Randall began to stammer. "Why? Because she knows nothing about the issues, the thousands, no millions, at stake."

"Tess knows what's at stake here," said Marjory, quietly. She met Tess's eye. "Don't you?"

"Yes," said Tess, her voice breaking. She couldn't believe it. Mom was taking her side.

"Mr. Mayor," continued Marjory. "I have supported my brother in his views on development ... until now. The death of that crane should be a warning to us."

"Where's that petition?" shouted a farmer at the back. "I'm putting my signature on it."

A man beside him stood up. "That crane's just like those canaries the miners took with them into the mines. They knew that if the birds died, the air was toxic."

"Let's not panic," said the mayor. "I want to get the facts straight. Now, young lady, where did you find the crane?"

"Near a drainage ditch down by Sandhill Resort. The water from the resort runs into that ditch," said Tess.

"I hope you're not going to take her word for it," said the company man.

"There are tests to determine the crane's cause of death," said the mayor. "We have the pellets the crane ingested and we know what pesticide the resort was using." The mayor gave Tess a kindly look. "But we'll need the bird for a day or two to run the tests."

Tess gripped Tabi tighter. She felt a hand on her shoulder. It was Clara! She had come to the meeting after all, despite her grief.

Clara hugged Tess, whispering, "Brave girl. Brave girl."

"They're going to test Tabi for poison," said Tess, blinking back tears.

"It's okay," said Clara. "It's okay. We'll bury Tabi later."

Tess took Tabi to the table. She lay the bird down, then removed her sweater and covered the crane's torso and his long skinny legs.

"Meeting's adjourned," said the mayor, "until one week from today."

Her mother came up behind Tess and wrapped her in her arms.

"Thanks," said Tess, and she burst into tears.

Under the Willow Tree

TWO DAYS LATER, just before sunset, her mother drove Tess to Clara's cabin. Clara had invited Tess over to bury Tabi. She was also invited for a sleepover. It would be like a wake, Clara had said.

"What's a wake?" Tess had asked.

Clara told her it was a party given when someone special died.

The air was hot and still. They drove past fields of blueberries, corn, and acorn squash, and farmhouses draped with beds of petunias and fuschias and marigolds.

"Losing Tabi's going to be hard on Clara," said Tess staring out the window.

"On you, too," said her mom.

"Yes, but worse for Clara," said Tess. "Tabi was her pet for fifteen years."

"You know, I never had a pet," said Marjory.

"Never?"

"My mother didn't care for animals," she said. "They dirtied the house."

"That's what you said to me when I asked for a pet,"

said Tess.

"Did I?"

"Yup. Exactly the same thing."

Marjory shook her head, then smiled.

"I guess I take after my mother more than I thought."

In the distance, Tess noticed that the sky was bright red with pale gold streaks.

Red sky at night, shepherd's delight. Grandpa's words.

When they reached Clara's cabin, Tess asked, "What made you change your mind about development?"

Her mother sighed.

"You'll think I'm crazy, if I tell you."

"You're one of the least crazy people I know," said Tess.

"Something happened when I saw you carrying Tabi. I remembered something, something I didn't want to. I remember my father carrying Hans's body from the slough. Water was falling from his clothes. His hair was pressed to his head. My mother was screaming. My dad was crying. When I saw the rain dripping from Tabi's wings, it was as if somehow the crane and my brother were connected. Then something happened in my mind which I don't understand ... a door opened to part of me I'd locked away. And I realized that when I lost my brother, I lost some of myself — the part of me capable of loving the marsh and all the birds in it. Until that moment, I thought it was my mother's protectiveness that kept me from the marsh, but it was more than that. It was my own fears. I was afraid that I might die out there, like my brother. But when I saw you carrying Tabi, I thought that, maybe, through the cranes, I might find myself." Marjory looked embarrassed. "It's hard to explain."

"It makes sense to me," said Tess, softly. "I think you're the best mom in the world!" She took her mother's hand and gave it a squeeze. "But Uncle Randall must hate you now."

Her mother laughed. "Randall's bark is worse than his bite. He can never stay angry too long. I was talking to him an hour ago. He was as happy as a loon."

"Why would he be happy?" asked Tess.

"Western offered him a job in their Seattle office. They told him they were impressed by his 'style.'"

"You're joking!" cried Tess.

"I'm perfectly serious," said her mom.

"But Seattle's in the United States. He'd have to move there."

"Yes," said her mom, "and he's thrilled. He's agreed to let me buy him out gradually."

"You mean Willowcreek will be all yours?"

"Ours, Tess. And yours, someday."

"Oh, Mom," said Tess. She wanted to laugh and cry at the same time.

"Sally's at the window. You'd better not keep them waiting."

"Do you want to come in for awhile?" asked Tess, shyly.

Her mother shook her head. "Tabi's burial should be for family members only. Besides, you and I will have lots of time together. If I'm going to be a birder, I'll need someone to teach me."

"*You're* going to be a birder?"

"And why not?" asked Mom. "I'm the eldest daughter of Edwin De Boer. Birding's in my blood! Though I don't know an owl from a hawk."

Tess smiled, leaning into the car.

"Bye, Mom."

"Goodbye, sweetheart."

Tess stood on the sidewalk and followed her mother's car with her eyes until it was out of sight. It was as though suddenly she and her mother were seeing each other for the first time. At the meeting, when her mom said, "Tess knows what's at stake," she'd heard pride and love in her mother's voice.

When Tess walked inside the cabin, Sally and Zak gave her a hug.

Then Tess went over to Clara.

"How are you doing?" she asked.

"I'm a sentimental old bird," said Clara, dabbing her eyes. Her eyes were red from crying. "I'm sure going to miss Tabi's antics. There was never a dull moment with that bird around. But I've got too much to do to feel sorry for myself. Miracle never stops eating and I've got to get out and see the wild downy."

Clara's face looked pale, but she hadn't lost the brightness in her eyes. She said, "Last night I dreamed that Tabi joined the wild cranes."

"Maybe he did," said Tess.

Zak was waving the newspaper. "I have something to show you."

"Oh?"

"You're on the front page."

The photograph showed Tess laying Tabi on the table, while the mayor looked on.

CRANE INCIDENT DEALS BLOW TO WESTERN

Tess De Boer, twelve-year-old granddaughter of the late Edwin De Boer, a pioneer who helped build the dyking system in the Pitt Polder, carried a dead crane into the Pitt Meadows council meeting last Thursday. De Boer found the crane's body near a drainage ditch close to Sandhill Golf Resort. She charged that the use of pesticides by the resort had caused the bird's death. The crane, called Tabi, was a pet belonging to Clara Williams, known to locals as the bird woman. An extensive battery of tests ordered by Mayor Davis has confirmed that the crane died of pesticide poisoning.

Zak McIver and Sally Pierre, along with De Boer, rallied the community to their cause. The grade seven students collected over 500 signatures on a petition to defeat Phase B.

There is speculation that Mayor Davis, up for re-election in late fall, intends to make the proposed development an election issue. The mayor is quoted as saying, "Over my dead body will Phase B pass." Bad news for developers. Good news for environmentalists.

"Wow," said Tess.

Zak took her hand and squeezed it.

"You did good."

Tess blushed. "Thanks."

"The mayor's discovered a way to be a hero," said Clara. "He's going to save the polder and win the election."

"Some hero," said Zak under his breath.

"It will soon be sundown," said Sally, standing at the window.

"Yes. Time to say goodbye to Tabi," said Clara.

"Where are we going to bury him?" asked Tess.

"Under the willow tree," said Clara. "I hung some cloth over the plastic door on Miracle's box, so we won't have to wear our crane suits."

Outside the back door, sat a long slender cedar box.

"That's Tabi's burial box," said Sally. "I worked on it for the past two days. It felt good to make it."

Tess knelt down before the box. She ran her fingers over the sanded corners and the scent of oil of cedar drifted up to her.

"The two half-diamonds joined means eternity," said Sally. "The carving's not very good. I'm just learning."

"It's beautiful," said Tess. "Is Tabi inside?"

"Yes," said Clara.

They carried Tabi in his box to the willow tree. From where Tess stood, she could hear the soft trickle of the slough, Swaneset's gift to the polder. And beyond that stretched the marsh, golden in the fading light.

They each took turns digging Tabi's grave. And when they lowered the box, they covered it with the rich black soil of the wetlands.

Clara took a small root of hardhack and planted it on the mound of earth.

"So Tabi can feel at home."

Sally built a fire in a circle of stones around which they sat. Then they honoured Tabi with stories, while the sun fell slowly behind the mountains and the coyotes howled and a marsh wind moved through another hot summer night in the polder.

· 32 ·

A Different Season

By EARLY SEPTEMBER, the blackberries had ripened in the thickets. Cattle grazed in warm fields and bales of hay were scattered like bolts of golden yarn. As the days grew shorter, the warblers, the yellowthroats, and the hummingbirds began to migrate south.

Miracle began rooting in the mud for worms. And catching dragonflies became her favourite sport.

"It's a good thing she's beginning to fend for herself," said Clara to Tess. "Now that school has started, we could never have kept up. That crane's eating three hundred worms a day!"

Miracle had grown rapidly during the month of August. She was now almost as tall as Tess. Her long legs had changed from a tawny pink to a dark greenish black. Then the crane began to moult — first, her head and neck feathers and later, those from her wings and breast. By the time her feathers gradually grew back, Miracle no longer resembled a chick.

"She's a juvenile now," said Clara.

"But why isn't she dancing?" asked Tess. "The most

she's done is a few bobs and the occasional twirl."

Clara shook her head. "I'm not sure, but cranes bond by dancing. If Miracle's going to take a mate, she'll need to learn."

"Then I'll teach her," said Tess.

"Crane dancing is instinctual," said Clara. "You can't actually teach her, but you could encourage her."

So every day after school, Tess changed into her crane suit and took Miracle to the meadow to dance. It was during these times that Tess missed Tabi most. She had loved dancing with Tabi. But Miracle seemed uninterested. The bird just stared at Tess, then went back to rooting.

One day, during a dancing lesson, Tess forgot about Miracle. She forgot about her school and her homework and friends. She thought only of Tabi, and how much she missed him. She turned slowly in her pearl-grey gown, waving her wing mitts, as she whirled and leaped and bowed. And as she danced, something seemed to catch fire in her. She felt lighter than air; she felt like flying.

Suddenly, she heard a high shrill peep.

Tess turned to see Miracle bobbing up and down on her long skinny legs. The young crane looked wobbly at first, then she seemed to gain confidence, bounding higher with each try. Tess held her breath. Miracle began to fan the air with excitement, then attempted an awkward twirl and a dizzy leap. Then lowering her head, Miracle bowed gracefully.

Tess leaped with pleasure. Miracle had finally learned to dance!

Clara came by in her crane suit. The bird woman stopped in her tracks. Tess heard a soft chuckle from beneath Clara's crane suit. Then all three of them danced.

A few days later, her mother suggested that Tess take her to the blind to see the wild cranes. They arrived at the blind around six in the morning and an hour later Marjory saw her first young crane. To Tess's surprise, her mother was thrilled. She asked a million questions and several times later that week, Tess saw her mother reading Grandpa's field guides.

"What are you doing?" asked Tess.

Marjory gave Tess a secretive smile and said, "I've got some catching up to do."

From then on, Tess took her Mom to the blind on weekends. They'd take hot chocolate, binoculars, and a spotting scope and they'd watch the crane pair and their young. One day, Marjory came home from town with a brand new pair of binoculars and a khaki-coloured birding jacket with lots of pockets.

"What do you think?" asked her mother, whirling around.

"It suits you," said Tess. And she suddenly realized it did. Her mother was becoming a birder.

As the weeks passed, the cottonwood leaves turned from green to gold. Then they fell from the branches, forming deep piles around the tree trunks. The leaves of the blueberry bushes turned a bright crimson. By mid-October, the rains grew heavier, swelling the sloughs and plumping the land with moisture. Mists hovered above the dykes and people spoke of polder ghosts once again.

The wild cranes of Willowcreek were getting restless. The crane pair had taught their young one to fly several weeks ago. They kept circling the slough, whinnying and flapping their wings.

"They're anxious to migrate," said Clara.

Tess was worried. Though Miracle had begun to exercise her wings, the crane still couldn't fly. And if Miracle couldn't fly, she'd remain dependent on humans to care for her. All their efforts would have failed.

One morning, Tess rose to see a fresh blanket of snow on the Golden Ears Mountains. She shivered at the sight. Snow in the mountains meant that winter was approaching. And that meant that any remaining cranes in the polder would soon migrate.

Tess bundled up in a warm jacket and walked over to Clara's. Miracle greeted Tess with a purr. Tess leaned towards the young crane and purred back.

"Let's go for a walk," said Tess, as she took the crane across the frost-covered meadow. A cold wind blew bits of dead vegetation across their path.

Halfway across the field, Tess stopped. A coyote was standing by a thicket. The animal looked thin and hungry. Suddenly the coyote lunged towards the crane.

Miracle didn't move.

Run, Miracle, run. A coyote is a predator.

Then Tess realized that a crane mother would have taught her offspring fear. But Miracle hadn't learned that lesson.

Miracle let out a shrill peep and faced the animal. Spreading her wings, she stabbed the ground with her bill.

Good. That's aggressive behaviour. Now you know the coyote's your enemy. But a wild crane would take flight.

Tess began to run, hoping Miracle would try and escape. She held her breath as she ran, afraid to look back.

When Tess turned, she saw Miracle take a running leap into the wind. The crane rose awkwardly into the air, beating her wings excitedly and peeping loudly.

Miracle's instinct for survival had finally clicked in.

Tess felt like laughing out loud. Miracle looked surprised at her accomplishment. She looked scared, too.

You've helped again, coyote. Though I'm not sure if you meant to.

The coyote gazed up at the crane for a few moments, then disappeared into the bushes.

For the next two weeks, Miracle was like a kid with a new toy. The crane spent hours taking off and landing, then she practised her turns. Even her rooting took second place to her enthusiasm for her new-found skill.

Then suddenly, Miracle began to regress. She clung to Tess, pecking at the feathers of her crane suit as she'd done when she was a tiny chick. She no longer seemed eager to fly. She seemed afraid to let Tess out of her sight.

"Maybe," said Clara, "she knows she's going to leave us soon."

A week later, Tess woke at dawn to the sound of crane calls. She ran to the window. Circling the slough, she saw a flock of wild cranes.

Quickly, she phoned Clara.

"There's twelve of them and they're calling to the crane pair."

"Just what we've been waiting for!" cried Clara. "Now where's my list? Phone Zak and Sally. Crane suit. Crane cage in pickup. Miracle in cage. Drive to slough ... I'll be there in fifteen minutes!"

"Yes!" cried Tess. Then she raced upstairs, pulled out her crane suit and a box from under her bed.

"Mom!" she called. "Come here! I've got a surprise for you."

Mom was still half asleep.

"What is it?"

"It's a present," said Tess.

"What's the occasion?"

"Clara's bringing Miracle over. Open it."

Her mother tore the wrapping off.

"A crane outfit?" She walked to the mirror, holding it up to her. "For me?"

"You earned it, Mom. All those mornings in the blind. I didn't want you to miss seeing Miracle off — if she leaves ..."

Marjory kissed Tess on the cheek.

"Thank you, sweetheart," she said. "I'll change right now. Now where did I put my binoculars?"

"They're in your raincoat pocket. Remember when you spotted that red-tail?"

"Dad's good-luck bird."

"We'll need some luck this morning," said Tess, pulling her crane suit over her head. "Clara keeps telling me, 'Don't get your hopes up.' I guess she's thinking about Tabi. She was disappointed so often."

"You've done your best, Tess. Every time you put on that crane suit you encourage her to be what she is ... a wild crane."

"I hope that's enough, Mom."

Tess sat by the window and waited.

The wild cranes were still circling and calling.

"Don't leave yet," she whispered.

Downstairs, Tess heard knocking, then voices. She ran downstairs.

Zak's and Sally's faces were flushed with excitement.

Clara was flapping her arms and talking fast. "Miracle's still in the truck. I've covered the cage with a blanket. Got your hoods ready? Glad to see you, Marjory. Nice looking outfit. Whoops, I almost forgot. One of us should lead our little one out. It's strange territory for Miracle. She'll probably need some encouragement. Any takers?"

"Tess should lead," said Zak softly. "This has been her dream."

"Yes, it has to be Tess," smiled Sally.

Tess's eyes met Sally's, and in a look, read her thoughts.

We are the crane sisters, honoured by the spirit of the crane.

Tess gave Clara a questioning look.

"It's settled then," said Clara. "Put your hoods on and let's go outside. Tess goes first, then the rest of us will follow in a single file. Keep your fingers crossed."

Clara lifted Miracle from the cage and placed her in Tess's arms. Tess held her closely for a few seconds. She could feel the crane's heart thumping through her crane gown.

Part of her didn't want Miracle to leave. Ever. But that was the selfish part of her. The better part of her would say goodbye, knowing she had done what was good for the crane and her species.

Tess placed her wing mitt gently on Miracle's crown. And suddenly, she felt three wing mitts around her own. Miracle's other foster mothers were saying goodbye, too. Then a fourth wing mitt touched hers. It was her mother. Beneath the crane suit, Tess met her mother's eyes. Her mom nodded at her, as if to say, I know how you feel.

Then Tess placed Miracle on the ground and began

walking towards the marsh. The crane clung to Tess's side, looking back every few minutes to her parade of foster mothers.

She's looking for reassurance.

As they neared the marsh, the wild cranes' calls grew louder. Sensing the flock's excitement, Miracle began to flap her wings and leap.

When the wild flock spotted Miracle, their calls increased.

"Come join us," they seemed to say.

Suddenly Miracle began to beat her wings rapidly, then she sprang into the air. She made a narrow circle a few feet above her foster mothers, then glided down beside Tess.

The calls of the wild cranes grew more frenzied and more insistent.

Miracle responded with an excited peep. The crane mothers stood still, afraid to move. Tess watched in awe as suddenly Miracle took several running steps and rose higher and higher into the air.

The wild cranes encircled the younger crane, carried her off with them in a burst of singing and Tess watched Miracle join her own kind.

Goodbye, beautiful bird.

Author's Afterword

Miracle at Willowcreek is a work of fiction, although it is based on reality. The number of greater sandhill cranes left in the Pitt Polder at the date of this writing is thirteen to nineteen. Each year, the crane population is declining. Crane behaviour, calls, and description of isolation rearing is factual.

The Pitt Polder is located in the northeast sector of Pitt Meadows. Forty-six kilometres east of Vancouver in the southwestern corner of the British Columbia, the polder is one of only two nesting places for sandhill cranes in the lower mainland.

The Pitt Polder continues to be under constant threat of development. In 1996, a proposal to locate a mega-theme park on the polder was under consideration, though negative feeling in the community resulted in its location elsewhere.

In 1997, proposed changes to zoning bylaws would have allowed a residential housing component and a hotel on a rocky knoll in the Pitt Polder. Though this proposed development would be located on the uplands of the polder, the opponents of the development believe that its presence would negatively impact the surrounding lowlands. Pressure from opponents resulted in the developer withdrawing the application, but this is most likely a temporary reprieve.

In 1998, the Pitt Polder Preservation Society and the Concerned Citizens for Pitt Meadows presented an initiative to prevent the repeal of a referendum bylaw by the municipal council, without holding a referendum. The municipal council has scheduled workshops and invited submissions on the bylaw from multi-stakeholders. The referendum bylaw would allow the citizens of Pitt Meadows to decide the fate of the polder.

In all likelihood, developers and landowners will continue to pressure municipal councils to build golf courses, condominiums, villages, and shopping centres on environmentally sensitive wetlands.

The Pitt Polder, Pitt Meadows, Sheridan Hill, and Pitt Lake are real locations. The flora and fauna referred to in this novel are accurate and specific to the polder, but many plants and wildlife may also be found in wetlands in other areas.

The Sandhill Golf Resort is fictional, as is the present location of the Katzie Reserve, which I changed to the polder from its real location in Hammond on the Fraser River. This change was made in recognition of the fact that the land now known as the polder is traditional Katzie land. Many of the sites, now developed, are still consider sacred by the Upper Stó:lō people. Sheridan Hill is only one such site.

The Katzie stories, told in the novel by Sally's grandfather and passed on to his granddaughter, are true renditions. The Katzie stories are based on the *Katzie Ethnographic*

Notes by Wayne Suttles and *The Faith of a Coast Salish Indian* by Diamond Jenness, first published in 1955 by the British Columbia Provincial Museum. They were last reprinted in 1986 together in one book. These are based on the oral history of Old Pierre, who at 75 years of age, had gained an honourable reputation as a medicine man, both on Vancouver Island and on the mainland. His son, Simon Pierre, also contributed to the history of the Katzie.

In the novel, Sally's grandfather is referred to as one of the "smokehouse people" rather than as a medicine man, because the Katzie do not have a word for the latter. *The Ethnographical Notes* do refer to Old Pierre as a medicine man, but this may only be Diamond Jenness's interpretation.

At many points during the writing of this novel, I was fascinated by the synchronicity between the plot of my novel and the traditional Katzie stories. I discovered, only after my writing, for example, that a guardian spirit is often handed down to a grandchild, particularly one who has suffered. In the novel, Sally has suffered from racism and Tess has suffered from the loss of her father and grandfather.

The characters in the novel are fictional, with the exception of the bird woman who is based on naturalist, crane researcher, and pioneer of the polder Wilma Robinson. Wilma has danced with the cranes, fed sugar "kisses" to hummingbirds, and has defended and mourned the gradual loss of our wetlands.

Glossary

Arum: A wetland plant also known as skunk cabbage or swamp candle. This large yellow lily-like flower with a strong smell appears in the early spring.

Bantam: A small breed of hen.

Blind: A structure built for the purpose of observing birds or other wildlife. It is often made of sticks, leafy branches, corn stalks, or brush.

Bog: An open, wet place with few trees. Bogs are poorly drained and covered with mats of moss. They contain acidic waters and specialized plants such as spaghnum moss, Labrador tea, wild cranberry, sundew, and swamp laurel.

Cattail: A perennial plant growing up to two metres tall with long narrow grass-like leaves, up to two centimetres wide, and a velvet brown cone-shaped flower spike. Cattails grow in marshes, ponds, and wet ditches. The plant provides important habitat and food for waterfowl and muskrats. First Nations people boiled the spikes and ate them like corn on the cob.

Carunculated: A description of the thick skin of a reddish colour on the head of the sandhill crane. This patch of rough skin has a few black hairs, but no feathers.

Cranberry: A bog plant with small pointed sharp leaves growing from long slender vines. Wild cranberries are often found growing among bright pink beds of spaghnum moss. When the berries first form, they are white. They gradually change from pink to crimson in the fall.

Contact call: The contact call is given by one crane pair member to the other, or by the parent to the eggs and the chicks. It sounds like a slow, low, soft purr. Contact calling stimulates the embryo to excercise and may be important to developing the strength of the chick.

Co-op: (short for co-operative) A place where the farmers sell their berries for a set price. The co-operative sells and ships the berries to various markets all over the world.

Devil's club: A tall plant with broad maple leaf-shaped leaves. The plant is armed with large yellowish spines that break off and fester if embedded in the skin.

Dyke: A bank of earth built up to hold back water. In the polder, dirt roads were built on top of the dykes, so people could walk along them.

Hardhack: A wetland shrub that grows one-and-a-half metres tall. Also known as pink spirea, it has large clusters of pink flowers that turn brown in the fall. The settlers called the bush "hardhack," because they had to hack through huge masses of the plant that readily took over wetland.

Labrador tea: An erect branching plant with leathery leaves. Thick rusty fuzz beneath the rolled edges of the fragrant leaf is a distinctive feature. In the summer, small white flowers appear on the bushes. The leaves make delicious tea.

Mandibles: The upper or lower segment of the bill of a bird.

Marsh: A type of wetland overgrown with coarse grasses, sedges, and rushes. Marshes are subject to periodic flooding. Water levels vary greatly.

Pacific Flyway: A geographic course along which birds migrate between wintering and breeding areas.

To pip: To break through the shell of an egg, as in hatching.

Reserve: A tract of land set aside for First Nations people under the Royal Proclamation of 1763. In Ontario and the Prairies, Aboriginal people signed treaties surrendering their land in exchange for specific compensation packages. However, the principals articulated in this proclamation were never applied in British Columbia. Only now are the federal and provincial governments beginning to negotiate with the Aboriginal people of British Columbia.

Slough (rhymes with "stew"): A creek in a marshland.

Smokehouse: A building used by First Nations people, usually built on the Reserve. First Nations people consider a smokehouse as a kind of church.

Swamp laurel: Also known as bog laurel or kalmia, this plant grows together with, and is similar to, Labrador tea, but does not have brown fuzz on the underside of the leaf. In the spring, swamp laurel has pink flowers while Labrador tea has white. Swamp laurel is poisonous, unlike Labrador tea.

Unison call: A duet exchanged by a nesting pair of cranes. The female emits two high-pitched calls for each single lower-pitched call. The calls are perfectly synchronized, so they sound like that of a single bird.

Updraft: An upward movement of air.

Wetland: Any area that is covered by water for a part of a day or year. Wetlands include floodplain, ponds, wet meadows, bogs, and marshes.

Glossary of Birds

Bald eagle: The largest bird of prey in Canada. It is about seventy-six centimetres in height and has a wing span of two metres. When the bald eagle is young, its feathers are brown. It takes about five years for a bald eagle to grow white feathers on its head and tail.

Barn owl: Sometimes known as a monkey-faced owl, because of its heart-shaped face and the absence of ear-tufts or "horns" of feathers. It nests in holes in barns, banks, or trees.

Bittern: Commonly known as the American bittern or thunder-pumper, because its distinctive *oonk-a-lunk* sounds like someone working a dry pump. The bittern hunts for frogs, fish, insects, young birds, and mice in bogs and marshes. When its enemies near, the bittern freezes, its mottled brown plumage providing an effective camouflage.

Black-capped chickadee: A small friendly, long-tailed bird with a black cap, black bib, and white cheeks.

Bufflehead: A stocky, short-necked, diving duck with a large puffy head and a short bill. The male has a black head with a white patch; the female has a dull brown head with a smaller white patch.

Canada goose: Canada's most common goose, the bird has a black head with a white chin strap extending from ear to ear. Its call is a low *honk-a-lonk.*

Cowbird: The male has a brown head and green body; the female is grey-brown. The female lays her eggs in the nests of other species of birds, such as sparrows, warblers, or vireos. The foster mothers bring up the cowbird's babies.

Crow: A black bird with a familiar *caw* call. Its fan-shaped tail in flight distinguishes it from a raven.

Dark-eyed junco: Juncos are common, rather tame sparrows, found in large flocks. The male is a slate-grey with a white belly; the female is a brownish-grey overall.

Great blue heron: This wetland bird is more than a metre tall. It has a black stripe on its head and a plume. When the heron flies, its neck is crooked, unlike the crane which flies with a straight neck. It nests in large colonies in tall trees and makes a hoarse squawking sound.

Green-backed heron: A small chunky heron that looks more blue than green. It has yellow or bright orange legs. This little heron will drop a feather or a leaf on the surface of the water for bait. When a fish rises to catch the artificial lure, the heron catches the fish.

Greater sandhill crane: A tall wetland bird with a wingspan of more than two metres. It has silver-grey feathers with a bright red patch of skin on its head. In the spring, the sandhill paints its feathers with the rust-coloured soil of the marsh. The sandhill flies with its neck and legs fully extended.

House finch: The male finch has a brown cap and ear patch. A stripe above the eye, the bib and rump are bright red. The females are a streaked brown. The song of the finch consists of three high-pitched notes, ending in a *wheer*.

Kingfisher: A blue-grey bird with a large crest on its head. Its head looks large compared to its body. The male has one ragged brown band on its chest; the female two. The kingfisher makes a loud high rattling sound as it hovers over the water, then dives for a fish.

Mallard: The male duck has a metallic green head, a white neck band, and a rusty breast. The female is a mottled brown. Its call is a loud *quack*.

Marsh harrier: A slim marsh hawk with long rounded wings and a long tail. It feeds largely on rodents.

Marsh wren: A brown solitary bird with a finely barred tail that is cocked upward and a slender bill. It has a loud scolding rattle.

Nighthawk: A kind of nightjar or goatsucker (see *nightjar*). Nighthawks differ from other goatsuckers in their long pointed wings, slightly pointed tails, and white patches on their wings. When the nighthawk dives, its wing feathers make a humming sound.

Nightjar: A family of birds composed of eighty or more species; also known as goatsuckers. These nocturnal insect eaters have large flat heads, small bills and huge mouths. At night, their eyes become huge and round.

Osprey: These large brown-and-white birds of prey build bulky nests in trees or on top of poles, near fresh or salt water. Their diet is almost exclusively fish.

Pine siskin: A rather tame finch that has a tiny patch of yellow on its wing feathers. Siskins often gather in flocks in coniferous trees. On the West Coast, it makes loud wheezy *shr-ee, shr-ee* sounds.

Violet-green swallow: From the head to the rump, the bird is a rich bottle green, washed with violet. The rump and tail is a dark glossy violet. The swallow nests in hollow trees or rock crevices.

Virginia rail: An uncommon and secretive wetland bird with a short neck, long legs, and long toes. Its call is a series of *kid-ick kiddick* notes.

Red-breasted sapsucker: This woodpecker has a red head, breast, and nape. It uses its sharp beak to drill holes in trees searching for insects.

Red-tailed hawk: A soaring hawk with a robust body and a fanned tail. The upper tail is reddish, while the under tail is pink. The hawk preys on rodents. Its call is a high faint scream.

Red-winged blackbird: These blackbirds nest in marshes and fields. The male is shiny black with red shoulder patches. The female is dark brown with streaks. Its song is a squeaky *kong-ka-ree.*

Robin: A common grey-brown bird with a red breast. It eats worms, insects, and berries. Its song is a *cheerily-cheer-up cheerio.*

Ruby-crowned kinglet: A tiny plump greyish-olive coloured bird that prefers conifers. The male has a bright red crown, often difficult to see.

Rufous hummingbird: This tiny colourful bird, common to British Columbia, hovers over flowers to sip nectar with a needle-like bill. The male has a reddish-brown back with green patches, green crown, and throat feathers of iridescent orange-red.

Snow goose: A large white goose with black wing tips. It breeds on the Arctic tundra, but is seen in winter on coastal wetlands.

Starling: A dark chunky aggressive bird with speckled feathers. It looks a bit like a short-tailed blackbird. It imitates the songs of other species.

Trumpeter swan: A large swan sometimes found along the West Coast during winter. Immatures have grey-brown plumage, changing to white after the first year. Its call is a double honk.

Yellowthroat: These yellow-breasted birds have an olive coloured crown, back, and wings. The male has a black mask; the female has no mask. Yellowthroats nest on the ground in grassy fields or marshes. Their song is a *witch-ety witchety*.

Warbler: A large family of birds, including sparrows, orioles, and wood warblers. *Wilson's warbler* (see below) is an example of a species within the warbler family.

Widgeon: A common duck that feeds mainly on aquatic plants. Widgeons fly in large tight flocks, unlike most ducks that fly in an open V.

Wilson's warbler: A bright yellow bird often found in willow thickets or bogs. The male has a shiny black cap; the female a yellow forehead. Its song is between fifteen and twenty high musical chips.

Leonard R. McGregor

A teacher, naturalist, and environmentalist, ANNETTE LeBox lives in British Columbia near a marsh that is home to an abundance of plants and wildlife, including greater sandhill cranes. She has written two picture books, *The Princess Who Danced with Cranes* and *Miss Rafferty's Rainbow Socks*. *Miracle at Willowcreek* is her first novel.